Thank Y(ou for)
the journey.

— G. Dedicke

Abel's Burden

By
Gregory Dedicke

Copyright © 2019
Written by: Gregory Dedicke
Published by: Take Me Away Books, a division of Winged Publications

This book is a work of fiction. Names, characters, places, and incidents are the product of the author's imagination and are used fictitiously. Any resemblance to actual events, locales, or persons, living or dead, is coincidental.

All Rights Reserved

Science Fiction

Space Fiction

ISBN-13: 978-1-947523-57-9
ISBN-10: 1-947523-57-0

Acknowledgments.

I want to give special thanks to:

My mother, for her love and support in everything I do.

My father, for giving me the courage to write this story.

My sister, for always being there to tell me how it is.

The publishers and artist for making this dream a reality.

To Linda, a sweet lady, for giving me guidance along the way.

My friends for their overwhelming support.

And of course, to you. Thank you for joining me on this journey.

Chapter 1

The roaring of dragon fire falls from the heavens through the clouds. This must be what angels felt like when they first descended from the heavens to carry out the wishes of their creator.

The pilot grits his teeth, his hands white-knuckling on the joystick and throttle. Entering a planet's atmosphere always feels as if he were free falling into a dead ship. Yet, he has done this thousands of times, and the rush never fails to bring a smile to his face. He can almost feel the heat of the fireball his ship created. Entering a new world always has its own little test. Survive the descent and explore the mysteries of the surface, whether already discovered or not.

Eventually, the fireball retracts, and the ship begins to steady once it acclimates to the atmosphere. Roaring turns into whistling of the wind, and depending on the density of the clouds, one can see the surface of the world.

In the case of Aegis 12, that world is toxic.

The pilot steadies his ship over the barren landscape that is Aegis 12, a planet in a back-end system barely within the grasp of humanity. The landscape looks like the surface of heavily rusted metal, with no structures and almost no vegetation. If this place ever knew the true potential of life, those days are long gone.

Funny, the lifeless planets bring the most opportunities and the most everlasting peace. Dead and forgotten worlds have stories; they have history, and history brings items of interest. Items that tell stories to those willing to listen, willing to study. For the pilot, those stories mean profit. The life of a Collector may not be the first choice for most people, but for this pilot, that life called to him from an early age.

That same calling brings him to this toxic, radioactive planet that may or may not have the ruins of a long-gone civilization. Although his lead sources are solid, worlds this dangerous tend to be the end for many Collectors, but those willing to take the risk usually reap the most lucrative rewards.

The pilot has his lead marked in the navigational system. Gliding through the planet's atmosphere for a few minutes should lead him to the top of the site. Along the way, he can feel the winds of the hazardous world, the gods here displaying their wrath differently. Lightning pierces its way through the rusty clouds and the winds push against the ship, as if trying to tell the pilot to turn back.

Although the realm of nature is convincing, the realm of man has always dominated the mind of the ambitious, and the ambitious measure themselves in wealth rather than well-being. Displays of wrath such as this world offers never dissuade the pilot. In fact, he relishes these threats. The thrill of the hunt and the reaping of the spoils justify any suffering of the journey.

The planet is trying to manipulate his ship. Every world is different, like meeting a new person. You have to get an idea of the way they talk and view things, and thus control the fluidity of the conversation. For the pilot, flying into a different world is no different. He figures out how the winds play currents, and he responds by manipulating his ship to ride them.

A ping sounds in his navigational system, announcing his arrival at his destination. As soon as he hears the ping, a clearing appears in a valley. As he approaches, the clearing solidifies, and the jagged mountains outlining the valley provide cover from the intense winds. Although the turbulence intensifies from the disruption of the mountains, the cover from the elements make it a keen landing site.

The pilot decreases altitude and picks his landing spot, moving his ship toward his target. The air whistles around the ship as he turns the vessel to glide downwards. As soon as he senses the ground's closeness, he engages the landing gear and feels the ship give a light shake. Now, with great care he slowly lowers the ship closer and closer to the ground until he feels the landing gear kiss the toxic surface.

Another successful landing. The homecoming test has been cleared. Now he must face the wrath of the planet in person, but the first steps are usually his favorite part. Besides finding the items that will bring him fortune, of course.

He unbuckles himself as soon as the whirring of the engines die down. He lifts his achy body out of the pilot's chair and rings the hallways of his ship with the clank of his boots. In order to survive, he'll have to put on his E.V.A. (extravehicular activity) suit.

The pilot moves into the storage bay and unlocks one of

the E.V.A. lockers. The suit fits over his oil-stained jumpsuit. He locks the buckles around his wrists and ankles, sealing key areas of the suit. Satisfied with the fit of the suit, he heads to a kiosk in the wall housing a small sphere. The pilot presses a few keys on the kiosk, and the sphere emits light from its center, as if waking up. Slowly, it removes itself from the wall by hovering close to the pilot.

"Rise and shine, Cleo." The pilot speaks to the sphere, like it's his child.

Cleo almost seems to blink. Then she emits a holographic body surrounding the sphere, lighting up the storage bay with its shape. The holographic shape takes the form of a parrot, constructed of illuminated particles. Cleo, the ship's artificial intelligence, is the pilot's essential helper and greatest friend. Cleo may be the size of a baseball, but her usefulness compensates for her size one hundred times over. The pilot needs Cleo not only for navigation, but for emitting light in dark and dangerous places, linking to the ship and keeping track of his vitals. Yes, Cleo is his closest friend.

The pilot moves to the rear end of the ship where he prepares to make first contact with the hazardous outdoors of Aegis 12. He heads to the bay's airlock and stands between the two doors. The open one leads to the inside of the ship, and the one in front of him is closed.

Cleo hovers close to his shoulder and he gazes down at a data pad on his left gauntlet. The illuminated screen shows the controls on his suit. He taps his index finger on a key and feels the back and chest plate of his suit jerk. Two metal stems from the chest bring the two pieces of his helmet together. A glossy helmet with a hose attached to the life-support battery on his back encase his head like a cocoon.

For a moment, the pilot sees nothing but darkness. Then the metal walls of the airlock return to his vision, and he hears his modulated breathing coming from the helmet.

"Cleo," The pilot commands. "Systems check."

He witnesses the heads-up display through his visor display. A red tinted list displays to the left of his view. One by one he watches the list turn green.

Life support... online

Vital signs... stabilized

Oxygen levels... satisfactory

As Cleo progresses through his systems check, the pilot opens a cabinet in the airlock. He snaps a pill-sized canister to a mount below his life-support battery, then he snaps a tool belt containing landing gear and other implements around his waist. Finally, he adds a compact and slick energy pistol with a battery cell in front of the trigger guard.

The pilot clasps the handgrip and performs a function test on the weapon, reading the etchings on the side of the slide, Apex-19. Satisfied with the functions check, the pilot holsters the weapon on his tool belt. He pivots toward the closed bay door. The list on the left of his view is now all green. "Cleo, are we good?"

Cleo beeps in confirmation, sounding as ready as the pilot. Fortune awaits.

"Good, let's do it. Seal the airlock and depressurize." The pilot's modulated voice rings through the bay's airlock. With that said, the door behind him shuts, and loud hissing fills the airlock. The pilot can feel the oxygen leak out of the room, waiting anxiously for the process to complete. After a few seconds, the door in front of him opens.

The radioactive winds strike the pilot and Cleo, almost knocking them back. They feel the wrath of the planet firsthand. Particles of dirt, dust, and sand strike his visor, sounding like a tilted rain stick. The pilot shields the front of helmet with his hand, blocking the nearby two suns and the particles being carried by the wind.

Time to step into this world. He descends the ramp of the ship, the well-worn ramp creaking below his boots.

The pilot steps off the ramp and is surprised to find the sand to be ankle-deep. The toxic sand builds up against the pilot's legs as he scans the landscape. Cleo hovers effortlessly with her holographic parrot body. Thanks to the brightness of Cleo, the pilot can find his way through dark places and heavy storms with low visibility, such as this one. This windstorm hasn't stopped since he broke through its atmosphere. Whether it's the normal environment of Aegis 12 or he caught it during a rare storm, it is unclear. Either way, this world seems angry.

The pilot trudges through the sands, evidence of his footsteps quickly blown away behind him as if the planet wants to erase all traces. He glances back at his research ship. Good thing it's designed to handle harsh environments and travel long distances by a one-man crew, although it was originally meant for four. The silver exterior of the ship is still visible through the harsh storm, with its aerodynamic construction and its wings retracted. The cockpit's glass is tinted as dark as night, and light from the two suns reflect off the glass, piercing the pilot's eyes through his visor. The engines are tucked under the folded wings, almost cold from inactivity. Even through the sand blasts and the wind, the pilot can still see the name of the ship inscribed on the side, *The Tip of the Spear*.

He turns around to scan the landscape. Not an easy task as his visibility is most likely ten meters. Trying to find the entrance to the site will be difficult in this weather. Luckily, Cleo is well lit and starts making her way to the entrance of the site. The pilot carefully treads through the sand, following Cleo, whom he hopes will lead him to the aperture of a cavern.

The sand may be loose, but it's almost as if it wants to stall the pilot. It swallows his ankles like quicksand, trying to drag him below to join those who dared to tread this same surface. But the pilot is not easily convinced. He swings his arms to give him momentum, and he kicks his knees high to conquer dunes building around his legs. Even with the E.V.A. suit assisting him with mobility, his muscles burn. *Is this the effects of radiation, or do I just sit too much on the pilot's chair?* Despite his thoughts, the roaring winds of the angry planet pierce his mind, making it difficult to think.

Finally, Cleo's light flashes next to a dark shadow on the side of the mountain. No, not a shadow, but the entrance. The pilot picks up his pace, pushing himself to make it to the shelter with Cleo.

Ten meters… five meters… and finally he feels his gauntlet rest on the rocky face. He then uses the surface to guide him toward the entrance. Once he steps into the cavern, the harsh winds of the world outside dissipate, and his body sags in relief. The burning in his muscles slowly fade away, and they relax from the labor. His breathing slows and becomes steady. He hunches his body and rests his hands on his knees, then straightens up to gaze into the darkness.

Cleo is bright, filling the immediate area around them with light, pushing away the darkness. Despite the small circle of brightness, the darkness outside their sphere closes in on the pilot. Darkness is always unnerving. Although his adrenaline pumps whenever he explores the unknown, based on his experience, the darkness hides the unknown's worst secrets. The pilot begins to breathe heavily again. The wind outside of the cavern howls behind him and the darkness of the cavern in front is almost speaking to him. The planet doesn't want him here.

He reaches to the side of his helmet and turns on his light. After a loud click, a beam of light pierces through the darkness. The light reveals rock, minerals, the glint of moisture reflecting off the rockface, and a pathway further into the cavern. Yet, most importantly, the whispers of the unknown world stop. At least for now.

He begins walking forward, the only sounds, his boots echoing and the slight humming of Cleo hovering close to his shoulder. Soon, the howls of the outside world become quieter as they travel further and further into the heart of the cavern. Despite the fading howls, the quietness of the caverns and the dripping of the water inside brings tenseness.

Goosebumps rise on his skin underneath his suit. His heartbeat picks up pace and he can feel the thumping in his chest. The evidence of his nervousness is apparent through his head-up display, as his vital signs show an increased heart rate. He hates the dark, despite his profession. Hate is his basic survival instinct telling him to turn back. Turn back, board *The Tip of the Spear* and blast away from this place.

No. He remembers one of his old mentors from when he first began this career. The pilot was young, barely out of the colony. That fear, that sweat, those second thoughts—these are the cost of fortune. He remembers the old man, closing in on his face, barking those words the first time he showed fear in a setting similar to this. Except that time, he was also in a group of juniors like himself. Such a mix of emotions they had—fear, excitement, and curiosity. They were all lead by the veteran Collector. An old man with a stout posture, his gray beard smelled like synthesized tobacco every time he screamed orders close to their faces. Funny, whenever the pilot feels fear, it's almost as if he can still smell that synthesized tobacco.

He remembers those other juniors. All young and naïve with clean faces and energetic bodies, ready for adventure. Yet he is the only one here in this cavern, still practicing his profession with a rougher face and more caution in his steps. The others either make their living elsewhere, have moved to other corners of the galaxy, or have paid the ultimate cost of pursuing their fortunes hidden in haunted planets.

Funny how in these dark places memories such as these spring up. The pilot continues to focus on the path ahead. Pressing his gauntlet against the rocky surface and using it as a guide, his helmet light shines a path forward.

The path seems to narrow. The walls of the cavern creep closer and closer together, trapping him between the cold stone. Eventually, the stone begins to separate again, and breathing becomes easier. These caverns are always unpredictable, and caution is the first thing a Collector learns during his first expedition. Caution is essential. Fortune laughs in the face of the reckless.

After a half hour of navigating the cavern, a light appears ahead. He is reaching his true lead. Hopefully a tunnel to a large space within the cavern, containing a terrestrial wreckage. The darkness retracts, and more light peers through the tunnels, until the pilot feels confident enough to shut his helmet light off.

He strides forward into the waking light and then he sees it. Beams of light shine down on warped wreckage. Metal warped like tinfoil, with what seems to be sails peeking out of the bundle of metal. Solar sails, the innovative work of ancient explorers long before the human race. Sure, humanity eventually utilized the idea of using solar sails to power their first colonizing expeditions, but these sails were cut with great craftsmanship. The ancient explorers who first utilized these created their ships with great love and care and saw astrological expeditions as a rite of passage. Spacecraft was not engineered; it was crafted like artwork.

The metal almost seems to be alive, with shades of green, orange, and yellow rippling through the surface. Starskin is the name Collectors gave this material, thought to have been crafted from minerals on an unreachable planet in another galaxy and infused with the energy of dying stars. Starskin has almost miracle-like properties with its construction, thus making it unbelievably valuable.

The pilot approaches to study the wreckage, his hands resting on his hips. This was a *Star Glider*. A craft used by a race way before humanity's time, but not believed to be native to the Milky Way galaxy. These beings took great pride in their exploration and astrological studies. Their knowledge allowed them to travel great lengths to another galaxy and travel to lengths still only dreamed of by humanity. These were true pioneers.

Odd, there are no biological remains of these travelers. Many theories suppose as to why, but all the pilot knows is these travelers alone set foot on Aegis 12. In fact, he may literally be the first human being to set foot on this terrifying and hazardous planet. As if that was an honor. To the humans centuries before, it may have been a great honor to travel this far. To a Collector, however, it is only necessary.

The pilot wastes no time. He checks his shoulder to see if Cleo is hovering close by. He spots her hovering close to a rock, taking the form of a hawk and scanning various pieces of the wreckage. Seeing that Cleo is ahead of him, he begins to scavenge through the wreckage for anything useful.

The Starskin metal alone is highly valuable—more valuable than what many Federation citizens make in their lifetime. The only issue is that it is damn near impossible to find a way to make it malleable enough to smelt it into concentrated ingots. Only these travelers knew how to process this material, but the methods of humanity didn't work. Still, their history and story alone provide great value to the higher class of the Federation, and he may know of some such buyers. The trick is finding pieces small enough to fit in his empty pill-shaped canister he carries on his back. He only has a ship, not any equipment to haul huge pieces of the wreckage.

The pilot lifts larger debris from the wreckage and sifts through for pieces that he'll be able to carry. Starskin is relatively light but carrying a large piece will prove problematic through the howling winds of the outside world. It's strange, since the winds are not apparent through the opening at the top of the cavern. The winds are actually due to the wreckage of *The Star Glider* because they have a unique effect on the atmosphere surrounding them. The air becomes still, heavier and even hums. The other Collectors believe that whatever Starskin is constructed of causes this. Either way, excavating these sites is always a treat for a Collector.

After searching the wreckage for a short while, the pilot

digs his gauntlets into the old sand and finds a piece of debris about a quarter of a meter long. He tugs the piece from the ground and lifts it up in front of his visor, with sand raining down from the debris. The Starskin debris is warped and crinkled like tinfoil, compromising its true appearance, but most pieces of this material are found like this.

Good enough. The pilot clicks the canister on his back. The lid opens from the side and he inserts the piece into the canister. He shuts the lid and seals it tight.

"Cleo, I think we're done here." The pilot's modulated voice rings through the cavern, and he usually hears a beep of confirmation in return. Yet this time, Cleo remains silent.

The pilot turns his head and looks around the wreckage. "Cleo?"

He searches the area. Cleo is not one to remain quiet. He shuffles through the still sand around the wreckage and spots Cleo hovering over debris, scanning the pieces of the wreckage. Yet, something looks odd. Cleo is scanning with great intent and curiosity. Then the pilot sees the source of her curiosity.

A bundle of bones.

The pilot treads over to the remains that Cleo is scanning. Could they have found biological proof of these explorers? That alone would be a more lucrative discovery than the wreckage. The pilot examines the remains. The corpse leans against a rock, baking in the sunlight and radiation. The dust smothering the bones make the pilot's nose twitch. The remains look familiar, very humanoid. Could the explorers of old be biologically similar to humans? He has to find out.

"Cleo, what's the result of the scan?" The pilot expects the results to pop in his heads-up display as unknown. But if these remains are not known and not human, then he'll have to contact some friends to investigate it further.

Cleo delivers the data back into the pilot's heads-up display: Species—*Homo sapien.*

Now, that is odd. As far as he knows, he is the only human that has laid foot on this planet's surface. He was hoping for biological evidence of alien intelligent life, but humans on Aegis 12 is still a startling discovery. The pilot stands over the dusty corpse, scanning it, starting from the feet.

He slowly moves his gaze up the corpse, "How did you die?" He asks as if the corpse would answer, almost humming the question under his breath. Bits of fabric are scattered around with the bones, giving no clear evidence of work or uniforms. Whoever this is, they have been dead a long time. Finally, when the pilot's gaze reaches the skull, the cause of death becomes obvious.

The skull of the remains has a hole in its forehead.

Even stranger. The pilot's mind is racing now. A slugger wound? To confirm his suspicion, he carefully moves the skull to examine the back of the head, and sure enough there is a larger hole with jagged edges, confirming that it is a slugger shot. If this was a suicide, then the angle of the shot placement would be extremely odd. No bullet entry from the side of the skull or an exit hole on the top.

This human, whoever it is, did not die of old age, radiation, or suicide. This human was murdered. The thought almost echoes in the pilot's mind. Not only that, this human was perhaps one of the only humans ever to set foot on Aegis 12, and that same human was also killed. The question remains, who killed him or her and why?

The pilot has broken through Aegis 12's atmosphere for

fortune, but he now feels something that he hadn't felt in ages—curiosity. Intense curiosity. Every Collector lead is a gamble. Yet, human remains on Aegis 12 calls for further investigating.

The pilot sets his gauntlets on his knees and rises to his feet, feeling a slight jolt of pain in his joints. The years of walking, climbing, exploring, and running on various planets have taken a toll on his body. He sets his hands on his hips and looks around the wreckage, then the remains. The hollow eyes stare back at him through his visor, as if death himself is watching him.

One thing is for sure. The remains, that skull, those hollow eyes—they have a story.

And to a Collector, those stories mean profit.

The storm breaking the atmosphere seems to be only the iceberg's tip.

The pilot evacuates the cavern shortly after his startling discovery, only to find the winds ravaging the landscape with the fury of angry souls. Cleo is also struggling against the furious weather, hovering against the wind while maintaining her holographic hawk body, only this time with a shade of crimson signifying extreme alert. As if that wasn't obvious given the circumstances.

The pilot struggles to maintain his balance. Even with his E.V.A. suit, these winds demand immediate shelter. Hopefully, *The Tip of the Spear* is anchored on the ground, so it won't blow away from this storm's wrath.

The pilot quickly thinks of what to do. Try to escape to the ship and risk getting lost in this godlike storm, or seek shelter in the caverns and wait it out. A high-pitched beep sounds in his heads-up display. Cleo is warning him of something.

An emergency message displays in the middle of his visor: Life support system low.

His life support. How could he forget? It's such a rookie mistake. A veteran like himself should've realized that the higher radiation levels would've drained his life-support battery faster. Once that battery depletes, his body will be cooking from the inside out and the outside in, with death laughing as the planet takes him. With that his decision is made.

"Cleo. " The pilot exclaims over the wind. "Pinpoint the ship." The pilot can faintly see the crimson hawk of Cleo strobing light from her holographic beak. It's not a perfect arrow, but it beats in this irradiated sandstorm. The pilot heads in the direction that Cleo is pointing. He shields his body from the wind, but the immense force almost pins his arm to his side. His muscles burn while he tries to shield his visor. At least that's what he hopes—that it is only the muscles burning from effort, and not radiation.

The pilot continues the trek forward, guided by his instinct and the dim strobing light. The planet is determined to hide his ship from him, but the pilot finds that if a person flies in one ship long enough, it becomes home. You can always find home no matter how dire the circumstance.

Soon enough, the pilot's instincts prove to be right. The faint shadow of the ship stands strong against the hellish storm punishing them. The pilot lets out a soft chuckle, but it is quickly silenced when his mouth stands agape and begs for air. Chuckling transforms into choking, and his vision tunnels and blurs until he sees the blatant emergency message. Life support battery depleted.

Desperation sets in, his throat swells, and he chokes from the empty space within his helmet. Suddenly, his skin burns, then immense nausea rises through his body and brain. Acid fills his mouth and his heartbeat races. The true wrath of the planet takes hold of the pilot.

Despite the seeming victory of the planet and death breathing down his suit , the pilot's legs somehow find their strength in the midst of his suffering. As quickly as the pain began, he lowers himself to his knees and crawls to the boarding ramp of his ship. Then he flips on his back while the door closes. The ramp shuts, and the chamber hisses like a snake, with the cleansing jets spraying over his body, washing away the toxicity of the outer world.

The pilot's E.V.A. retracts his helmet and oxygen finds its way back to his lungs. He gasps for air and gently touches the newly formed blisters on his face. His breathing steadies after a couple seconds of hyperventilating, and his vision blackens. Metallic arms spring out from the walls of the chamber and spray antiseptics onto his face, and the other arms cut his suit to access his wounds. With his consciousness fading to black, he hears the robotic but feminine voice of *The Tip of the Spear*:

"Welcome back, Captain Abel."

After those words of salvation, consciousness fails him.

Chapter 2

Abel opens his eyes, inhaling the clean air deeply through his nostrils. Oxygen. How often he's taken it for granted. After his experience last time with a malfunctioning life-support battery, inhaling the clean air of a remote planet can often only be described as...exhilarating. Not like home, not like the colony from which he was picked up, the air polluted with toxins and residue, the result of an industrial powerhouse. Not like the smell of rust and iron, of gasses and chemical aromas. Only the smell of clean, crisp air.

He gazes at the landscape before him. A land of beauty, a land of bounty. Flora is abundant through the hills. Tall trees reach toward the stars. Forest green moss coat the rocks, the blooming blossoms are as orange as a sunset, and the blood red vines of the trees tangle with the other vegetation and minerals. Before him lies a valley, which cuts through the plentiful gap in the surface, with the icy blue water bright amidst the vegetation.

Abel's foggy breath forms as he exhales, his lungs enriched from the cool atmosphere. His gaze shifts from the landscape up toward the stars. Dancing, colorful lights across the sky smother the cosmos. The air is quiet. He listens closely and swears he hears a subtle hum in the atmosphere. Here the angels whisper.

A moment ago, he was choking for air and his E.V.A. suit was being cut. Yet, rather than a heavy suit constructed of synthetic fibers and aluminum, garments of cloth and waxed canvas hug his body. His breath is steadied, his face is smooth and youthful. His energy is vigorous, and his eyesight is crystal clear. The dew of the air coats his slick, black hair and his sun-kissed skin. His scruffy beard is now shorter and prickly with stubble. His hazel eyes dance across points of interests throughout the landscape. This is his first time seeing anything as beautiful as Promethium.

Yet he has been here thousands of times. His youthfulness restored, and his actions not his own. This a memory, a cruel tease of a more pleasant and simpler time. A reoccurring dream that is so repetitive he is aware of it whenever he is unconscious. Yet he cannot control his actions within the dream. It doesn't matter. The sequence of events is the same.

"Abel?" The youthful voice breaks the humming silence and comes from behind him. He knows it's coming, yet he curses mentally every time. He can't seem to listen hard enough to focus on the humming and understand what it's trying to say.

Abel turns around to face the source of the voice. Another man is a little older than him, his face clean-shaven with shorter, brown hair damp from the air. His emerald green eyes return his gaze. He lugs a rucksack on his back and climbs the hill with labored breathing. Despite the heavy load, he carries it with exhilaration. Oh Ethan, always the try-hard.

"'s up, Ethan?" Abel replies with a hint of annoyance in his voice.

Ethan stops before the summit of the hill where Abel stands. "Big man says to set up the surveyor over the valley, and I figured this is a decent spot. What do you think?"

Abel turns to look upon the valley and returns his gaze to Ethan. "Good as any."

"Great." Ethan joins Abel on the peak of the hill and sets down the large rucksack. He drops to his knees and opens it, revealing a metallic, sphere-shaped contraption with sturdy legs. Lifting it out, Ethan places it on the soft ground and presses a button.

The contraption springs up off the ground, extending its tripod legs. A small dish appears on top of the machine and rotates while emitting a subtle beeping sound.

"That should do it." Ethan knocks the dirt off his hands and glances at Abel. "Can I ask you something?"

I know what you're going to ask. Regardless, his dream pushes on. "Yeah, what is it?"

"How did you join this crew? Or better yet, why are you here?" Ethan asks.

Abel opens his mouth to respond, but a rough yet profound voice answers the question for him. "He is here because he is like you—"

Both the young men turn their heads and see a much older man standing by the surveyor. He puffs out a large cloud of smoke, the smell of synthetic tobacco plaguing the air. A robusto cigar rests in his hand with his other hand on his belt, wrapped around a thick, knee-length coat with a fur collar. His dark eyes stare back at them, with the lights in the dark sky reflecting off his bald head and the gray beard framing his face. Despite his age, the man carries himself with confidence.

"Ambitious, curious, and a boy that came from nothing." The man ambles toward them, his height towering over their heads. Underneath his thick coat is an athletic build, uncommon for men his age. "Many of these fresh bloods come from broken planets. Lands with no opportunity and no future, plagued by disease and poverty. Yet they all desire something, whether it is glory, fame, fortune, power, or simply excitement. Nevertheless, it is ambition."

He moves between them, continuing his lecture. "None of you would be here if it weren't for me." He exchanges glances with the two young men, then focuses his attention on Abel. "What is it you desire, boy?"

Abel thinks for a moment, the humming of the air filling the void of silence. Then he returns his attention to the old man. "A future, Ser Kodak."

Kodak stares into Abel's soul with his dark eyes, taking in his answer. He lifts the cigar to his mouth and takes a deep puff without breaking eye contact, the foul-smelling smoke leaking through the small gap between his lips, then blows smoke into Abel's face. "We'll see."

Suddenly everything around Abel freezes. Ethan, Ser Kodak, the planet, the lights in the sky, and the air. Everything freezes. Abel peers around. A feminine voice whispers through the air:

"Wake up."

Abel bolts up with a gasp, eyes wide open. His body is cold, yet drenched in sweat. He finds himself back on *The Tip of the Spear*, his E.V.A. in pieces around him, as well as his base-layer clothing. He lies in the center of the bay chamber, naked and covered in blister scars. If it weren't for the ship's emergency medical system, he would've had a worse fate. Still, his body feels heavier than the ship. His mind feels dense and foggy, aware only of the metal surrounding him.

Cleo is nowhere in sight, most likely nested in her port within the ship. Abel takes a moment to muster the strength to stand. Barely escaping death has left his body weak and flimsy, the extensive emergency medical procedure has left him in aching pain, but he is alive. Collectors often don't experience the luxury of having such luck.

Abel spots his utility belt and the pill-shaped canister with his treasures inside amidst the pieces of his suit. The treasure and grim reminder of mortality—the human skull. He grabs both the belt and the canister and attempts to stand. His body must have added a few decades to his age; his muscles burn from the effort.

Once he stands his senses come back to him slowly. The ship hums from machinery and electronics, as it sits idle. Strange, the horrific winds from the outside world do not scream as loudly anymore, giving the inside atmosphere of the ship a more peaceful ambiance. The lights inside strike Abel's eyes, but then his vision returns to normal, since the ship is actually dimmer than when he initially woke up from his dream.

He has no idea how much time has passed, but often to a Collector who travels extensively, time is relative. Collectors do not recognize the time of night and day, only what is light and dark. They listen to their bodies, since they deal with multiple time cycles of various planets and solar systems. In the case of Abel's body right now, his body is begging him for rest.

Abel walks through the corridors of the ship. Despite the

superheated world outside, the ship and its metallic corridors are cold. The metal floors below him feel like ice against the soles of his feet. His stomach rumbles and his throat feels as dry as the arid atmosphere of Aegis 12. So many needs to address. So little energy to do so.

Abel enters his quarters. A small space with a simple cot, a wall locker and an ordinary desk. Not exactly luxury, but more than what he needs. He sets down his belt and the canister on the desk and makes his way to his wall locker. He opens it to change into a new set of clothes.

The door of the locker opening sends metallic ringing through his ears. The inside of the locker is dimly lit, revealing only a couple of jumpsuits, boots and a thick coat with a fur collar.

On the inside of the door hangs a photo of himself posing with Ethan and Ser Kodak standing among a large group of young Collectors. He slides into one of the oil-stained jumpsuits and pulls the boots on. The ship is cold, so he also grabs the thick coat. He slowly slides into its sleeves and buttons it up to his chest, the coat reaching down to his knees and the fur collar hugging his sore neck. A slight hint of synthetic tobacco strikes his nostrils.

He stands there, hugged by his clothes, staring at the old photo. Ser Kodak wears the same coat that is now on Abel's body. He breaks his gaze from the photo and kicks open a locker at the foot of his cot. The lid pops open to reveal a few bottles of water, non-perishable food and an almost empty bottle of whiskey. He snags a bottle of water and takes a few gulps, its wetness soothing his throat.

He turns to the container on the desk, pondering his next move. Curiosity returns, the human skull in a dead land, where no human being dares travel. He goes to the desk, tucks the container underneath his arm and heads to the center hub of the ship with the bottle of water in his other hand.

Abel sets the container on a table in the center of the hub and grabs a folding camping chair by the table. The minute he unfolds it, his body falls into the chair. He kicks his feet up and begins to plan.

"Cleo." Abel croaks. It's frustrating to him that everything now requires pained effort, at least for a while.

A blue tint hologram emits from the round table. Cleo is displayed as a housecat now, licking her paw.

"We need a plan." Abel speaks his thoughts out loud. "We need to find out who this skull belongs to. Where would we begin?" Abel takes another sip of water. The skull's age is unknown as well as its gender. Cause of death is pretty obvious, but other than that, he is lost about how to identify the skull. He needs to bring it to someone who can.

Since the skull is human, it could belong to a Federation citizen. The Federation governs almost all of humanity's existence across the cosmos and its colonies. Finding someone who can further analyze the DNA and cross-reference it with the citizen DNA registry could be a good place to start. There's no guarantee that the remains can even be identified but knowing who this is will help him solve this mystery.

Who could this be? And more important, why does he care? Is it worth the effort? Even if he finds out who this is, it's not like he plans to notify the next of kin. Although the Federation has citizens who go missing all the time. Finding those missing people can often be awarded with units, especially if it is someone from a wealthy background.

The skull could also belong to another Collector, and it

could lead him to another larger treasure on Aegis 12. And then there's the murder. Who killed this person and why? Could it have been another Collector who did this for the salvage? It doesn't happen often, yet it's plausible.

Abel's mind is flooded with these questions, then he turns his gaze to Cleo's cat hologram. "Cleo, please bring up the local system map."

Cleo's holographic-cat image stops licking its paw and stares back at Abel, then dissipates into cosmic disorder, its holograph separating like dust particles in the wind. Then the particles form into a pattern, imitating the stars, worlds, and other cosmic features that map out their present solar system. The Sovlikian System. A solar system on the edge of the Federation's influence.

"Cleo, highlight any Federation space stations within the system."

A small red light emits among the holographic particles and lands close to a planet known as Loberon, toward the center of the system. Data displays next to the red particle reads Station 17.

Only one station in the system. Most stations are quite large, yet this one is heavily industrial for its economy, and a poor economy at that. The chances of finding a forensic scientist there may be slim, especially one willing to help. Abel can't bring the skull to the authorities either, especially being a Collector. Finding a forensic scientist who's willing to help will be somewhat difficult.

But black-market scientists conduct illegal experiments in the Federation's territory. Yet, those people are not only hard to find, but expensive to enlist their help. Not to mention that most black-market scientists whom Abel has encountered in the past are sketchy characters, sometimes willing to inflict human suffering in order to conclude their experiments. Still, a poor space station on the rim of Federation territory will be a good place to start to find one. Either way, Abel now has a plan forming in his mind.

"Cleo, let's go ahead and plot a course for Station 17 next to Loberon." Abel pushes out of the flimsy camping chair and hurries to the cockpit. The star map's holographic particles form back into a cat figure, with Cleo sending off a positive beep in confirmation.

Abel's body falls back onto the pilot's chair, and he lets out a deep sigh. His body is finding its strength again. He taps the black navigational screen, which awakens the dusty monitor from its sleep. He studies Cleo's plotted course to Station 17. It seems to be a short trip, only a few hours to the station with the recently upgraded pulse engines.

Abel peers out at Aegis 12 one last time. The landscape still maintains its rusted metal appearance, with the exception of newly formed sand dunes, a result of the intense storm that almost took his life. While gazing at the landscape, Abel flips switches and manipulates controls around the cockpit. With each flip and button press, the ship roars to life.

The ship begins to shake, the whirring of the engines race through the corridors and cause the sound around the ship to clear, forming a crater within the sand. *The Tip of the Spear* now roars like a dragon, with the suns reflecting off the chromatic plating of the ship, almost as if forming their own star down on the surface.

Abel slowly pulls the yoke toward himself, and the ship begins its rise to the heavens. Thankfully, the winds are calm and don't pose a threat anymore, as if the planet is ushering him out. With a jerk of the controls, the ship points its nose toward the sky and throttles to join the stars.

The engines skirt the sand dunes across the surface and blasts off between two jagged mountains. The ship easily climbs altitude, scaling the sky on an easy slope. Soon, *The Tip of the Spear* pierces the rusty clouds and makes its final leg of ascent.

After a few seconds, Abel finds himself among the stars with the toxic world below him. Abel manipulates the controls to align the ship on its course. Abel eyes Aegis 12 one last time, then looks at the horizon. So many stars, so many worlds—endless possibilities.

Yet only one skull and one mystery.

Abel flips the switch for the pulse engines, and the ship beeps in countdown. The countdown emits its final beep and *The Tip of the Spear* blasts into the vast space. "Time to find answers," he whispers to himself.

Chapter 3

What were once little twinkles of light in a vast, empty space are now streaks of luminescence all leading to the center of Abel's view. Lightspeed travel, once an impossible feat for humanity centuries before, is now a common practice for any traveler. Still, the trip takes a couple hours to reach the space station. Meanwhile, Abel dances his fingers across a data-pad screen to research any leads that he may have.

"What do you know about Station 17?" Abel asks.

"Not much more than you." Cleo purrs her answer.

"What about crime rate? Or the black-market scene?"

"A moment." Cleo responds, followed by a few subtle beeps. "Station 17 is reported to be a hotbed for eco-terrorists. Many of them conduct their operations there."

"Eco-terrorists?"

"Yes, with the Satyr Militia being the main one. Still want to go?"

Abel only sighs as his response. Not an ideal first choice of a place to start, but he only has so much fuel and only so many ideas. Besides, he still has the Starskin debris piece to sell and he knows of a potential buyer. He's going to need those funds to purchase a new E.V.A. suit and to refuel. Even perhaps acquire some warp fuel just in case he has to jump to another system.

Security is going to be somewhat tight and the Federation is going to have some personnel patrolling the station. Not usually a problem, but he may have to be creative to reach out to any underground contacts.

A red light tints the cockpit, signifying the ship is about to approach the station. Abel sets down his data pad and clicks his seatbelt to prepare for arrival. He glances over to the navigational screen and sees the digital numbers counting down.

Three… two… one…

Suddenly, Abel's body is jolted forward, restrained by the seatbelt of his pilot's chair. His eyes lift to the glass of the ship's cockpit, and before him lies one of the most impressive feats of human industry.

A moon-sized station sits just above the atmosphere of Loberon, smothered with infrastructure and ships flying around the station like termites. Skyscrapers dot the station's surface, with metro transits running between the structures like veins. Ships line up for docking at various ports and a line of supply ships lift off from Loberon below. Flashes of light burst from Abel's left-side view. A Federation fleet arrives exiting lightspeed jumps.

Station 17—practically a man-made moon.

The ship's intercom erupts, first sounding static, then a man's tired voice breaks through the cockpit. "This is traffic control of Federation Station 17. Please state your credentials and business," The voice rings through the intercom, shrouded by static.

Abel presses a finger on the intercom to reply. "This is Captain Abel of scientific research vessel *The Tip of the Spear* reference number 16-13568, requesting permission to land for refuel and general errands." Then Abel lets his finger off the intercom.

"Stand by," The traffic controller replies almost immediately. A few seconds pass, then the intercom erupts loudly again. "Captain Abel, you are cleared for landing. Please proceed to dock ten for customs and please have your proper credentials ready. Welcome to Federation Station 17."

"10-4." Abel grips the controls and manipulates the ship toward dock ten. The station comes closer, and the vibrant life and industry takes on energy and color as he approaches the dock. Soon enough, Abel can see a landing pad with a large "10" visible on the pad, along with rhythmically strobing lights lighting the way. The ship slows its approach, but the landing gear causes the ship to jerk.

Perhaps it could use a quick oiling to make the landing gear engage more smoothly. Then the ship sits on the pad like a feather, and the pad descends into the station with bay doors sealing the ship as it descends into the heart of the station.

Flashing lights spiral through the cockpit among periods of darkness. Abel unfastens his seatbelt and bolts from the chair. He strides toward the quarters to prepare for station life. His first impressions: crowded, filthy, and just plain stressful.

He opens the wall locker in his quarters and grabs a simple messenger bag, constructed of olive-waxed canvas, along with leather padding on key areas of the bag. He slings the bag over his shoulder and walks over to the pill-shaped canister. It's too big to fit in the bag, so he opens the canister, letting out a soft hiss. He yanks the Starskin debris, and pulls out a smaller cube-shaped canister, containing the human skull. He stuffs it in his bag, along with a pack of synthesized cigarettes and a metal flask, as well as his credentials for customs.

He checks his utility belt, the Apex-19 pistol holstered on the belt. Due to the increased security, he doubts he'll be able to take it past customs, which only makes him more nervous. The descent of the landing pad stops.

Damn, what a long way down. Abel moves toward the closed boarding ramp of the ship. His hand forms into a fist, and he slams it against the ramp controls. With a soft hiss, the ramp opens, revealing a huge hangar with various captains, crew members, Federation guards, and passengers milling around the hangar. Other ships descend on other landing pads, varying from industrial haulers to economy-passenger ships. Meanwhile other landing pads return to the surface of the station.

Abel surveys the commotion. One can often tell the state of the station just by observing the hangar. All of the crew members of the ships are tired and unenthusiastic. The passengers wear work outfits, and they share the same disgruntled expressions on their faces.

Federation marines patrol the landing pads in squads, with 7.56-Valkyrie plasma repeaters slung across their bodies. The soldiers wear glossy, black armor from head to toe with the eyelets of their helmets emitting a flat, red line where their eyes would be. All of the soldiers wear a blue armband with the Federation's sigil, an eagle holding an olive branch and a lightning bolt with its talons, surrounded by a circle of thirteen stars. The emblem is reminiscent of the Earth-based states that originally founded the Federation.

Abel processes the information. Station 17 is struggling. It doesn't exude great economic confidence, and the business of the eco-terrorist is obvious due to the presence of the Federation's patrols. The people seem exhausted, beaten down with labor, and unhappy with their current position.

Cleo hovers by Abel's shoulder in the shape of a hawk, then Abel opens his bag for Cleo to nest in. With the little helper in his bag, Abel darts through the busy chaos of the hangars.

He bumps shoulders with workers and crew members every few paces, and the Federation marines eye him through their intimidating visors, just waiting for an excuse. Abel passes several docks with numerous ships dropping off different cargo. Mainly industrial haulers populate the hangars, making *The Tip of the Spear* stand out among the beaten ships.

Finally, Abel joins the customs line for entry into the Station 17. Judging from their attire, grisly characters wait for processing so that they can get to their jobs. Many workers transfer between stations and worlds, depending on their profession and industry. One thing is for certain though, the work is never done.

The line shortens every five minutes or so, until Abel is next in line. In that moment, he peers at the small data pad on his wrist to double-check his credentials.

"Next." A feminine but firm voice booms toward Abel, causing him to shoot a glance toward the kiosk. A simple kiosk lies in front of him with the holographic projection of a tidy Federation customs agent waiting for him. The holographic projection shows a young woman with a tight bun. Abel steps up to the kiosk with his wristband exposed.

"Please scan your credentials," The hologram commands, and Abel holds his wristband toward the scanner below the woman.

"Hold." The projection of the woman seems distracted for a moment, processing his scan. Then she glances up at Abel. "Clear, you may proceed." The gates in front of him swing open with a green-tinted light. When Abel steps through, a rapid commotion catches his eye. A crowd of Federation Marines rush past the gates toward a man who yells in pain.

A lone marine is jabbing a slick, black baton into the man's side, causing electrical shots to jolt throughout his body. The man twitches and falls to the floor, with the extra enforcers arriving to drag him by the arms to another area out of sight.

Abel breaks his attention from the scene and strides away from customs. *Not my business.*

The corridors off Customs might as well be a labyrinth, as Abel navigates his way to general transportation. Station 17 is a large space station, and he is going to need a place to come up with a plan to find someone who can analyze the skull.

He finds himself at a bullet train, with citizens flooding like ants in and out of each cabin. He takes in the environment. Bright and vibrant advertisements light up every cranny of the alleyways. Shades of dark and bright purple, crimsons and teals light up the pathways and show the details of the citizens' grizzled faces. The structures rise high into space while the metro trains rush through transparent tunnels wrapping around the structures. Ships speed around the structures, and sparks fly from distant construction projects.

Abel's vision begins to tunnel, and his heart rate beats faster. The crowds, the noises, the lights join to take a toll on a man who prefers to be traversing alone on uncharted planets—even planets such as Aegis 12 with its radiation storms. Still, the anxiety resulting from the constant organized chaos nags at his mind. They study him, wondering why he isn't covered in soot and stooped with exhaustion. Maybe they're measuring his privilege, deeming whether or not he is worthy of their time. Or perhaps they think he's an eco-terrorist.

Abel steps into the train with its horde of citizens. He focuses on the list of stops upon the screen and plans his route. If there's any place to begin his search, he knows just the man to point him in the right direction, the man who pointed him to the Aegis 12 in the first place.

Chapter 4

The scent of burning sage flares the nostrils and the smoke of incense fills the air. The room is dim, but light enough to check the listed prices.

The shopkeeper tends to his products, cleaning and rearranging for preparation of the next day. His large body waddles among the shelves, his breathing labored. Still, the scent of burning sage keeps his mind filled with purpose and relaxed with concentration. Even though the shop seems cluttered, he works hard to make sure there is comfort for his customers. One can only do so much to distract the mind from the rough industry outside his shop doors.

He stops to check his ornament by the register, a glistening, gold beckoning cat. Suddenly, the doors open behind him and the bell chimes. The shopkeeper doesn't break his eyes from the cat. "I'm sorry, but the shop just closed for the day. If you wish to come tomorrow, I can certainly help you find means of tranquility."

A moment passes, and the shopkeeper hears no reply. His nose picks up a different smell than burning sage—the smell of synthesized tobacco.

"Ah—" The shopkeeper turns around the see a tall, rugged man. Wearing a thick coat with his arms crossed, he analyzes his every move. "Good to see you again, Abel."

"Hello, Zao," Abel replies with a straight face, yet there's a hint of exhaustion and a few blister scars.

***

Zao adjusts his glasses and waddles closer to Abel. "I hope that you'll finally take up my offer for meditation. If not, then perhaps… another lead?" Zao plays with his fat fingers, analyzing Abel's eyes for his response.

Abel keeps his arms crossed. "You could say I need another lead."

Zao chuckles. "I imagine Aegis 12 was lucrative. You're already up and ready for another."

Abel scans the shop, analyzing the clutter. "I would say I have more questions than profit."

"Questions? Not another lead?"

Abel remains quiet for a moment and ambles over to the gold-beckoning cat, paying with its moving paw and not meeting Zao's eyes. "I thought I was the only one you gave that lead to."

Zao's chubby face scrunches. "You were. Abel, you know me," he replies with a hearty chuckle. "You're my favorite, so you get dibs on the good gigs."

Abel turns away from the cat and peers into Zao's small eyes. "I was the first?"

Zao steps back from Abel's tall body, towering over him, and frowns at the synthesized tobacco smell from his coat, disrupting his focus. "Y-yes, Aegis 12 only had drones scan it. In fact, you may be the only human to have dared traverse it… judging by the scars."

"Yeah, we'll get to that in a moment." Abel remembers

the planet roasting his skin, barely escaping with his life. Zao failed to portray the hostile environment of the lead accurately, which was also his fault, since he should've been more careful. "I'm here for another reason. I wasn't the only human to set foot on Aegis 12."

"That's impossible." Zao's face glistens with sweat. "Aegis 12's existence was known, but only explored with drones."

Abel steps away from Zao, pulls out his cube container and sets it on the shop counter. "Not exactly."

Zao examines the container and places his finger on the latch. The lid pops open, and the skull stares back at him with hollow eyes. Zao startles back from the sight. "Dear… Abel, why did you bring a skull into my shop?"

"Why do you think?"

Zao eyes it but stands back, as if it'll jump at it him or unleash a curse. "Wait, you found this there?"

"Yup, next to the *Starglider* wreckage."

"Wait, what?"

"You seem surprised, Zao," Abel's tone becoming firm. "I'm going to ask you again. Am I the only one you've sent to Aegis 12, or is it where you send all of the Collectors that you need to rid of?"

Zao scoffs at Abel's sudden questions. "What? Of course, you're the only one. And no, I do not send Collectors anywhere to get rid of them. Jeez, you're so paranoid. Like the rest of the lot in your… profession."

"I can say the same for your profession," Abel replies, his arms crossed, his back leaning against the counter. "Well, any explanation?"

Zao's posture begins to relax. "None. Who knows who this sorry lot is? And you said you found him next to the wreckage?"

"That's right. Another Collector maybe?"

"Maybe... Collector partnership? Had a disagreement over how to split the wreckage?"

"Perhaps, but the wreckage site didn't show signs of it being picked clean. In fact, quite the opposite."

"It was untouched?"

"As far as I know. Cleo found the corpse a few meters away from the wreckage."

Zao brings his hand up to his chins, and squeezes his jawline, deep in thought. "Abel, I have no clue how this could be possible. The Federation only learned of Aegis 12's existence a couple of Earth years ago." Zao waddles through his shop thinking out loud.

"How did you find out about the wreckage?" Abel interrupts his thoughts.

"I have an anonymous source in the Federation." Zao's voice becomes reluctant.

"Who?" Abel's voice rises.

"I can't disclose my sources. You know how it is. That's how we keep our lucrative gigs confidential."

Abel sighs. He hates red tape, but the Collector community is a tight-knit one. They're secretive of their gigs for job security, one thing that Abel clearly understands. He pushes his frustration aside for a moment and takes on a calmer tone. "Okay, so since you can't disclose your source, any idea who can help us find out who the skull belongs to?"

Zao's eyebrows furrow and beads of sweat form on his forehead. "Wait, we?"

"Yes, we. You promised that Aegis 12 was safe. It was nothing like you stated." Abel rubs the blister scars on his face. "You owe me this time, big guy."

Zao inhales through his nose and leans on the shop counter. "I may know someone who can help."

Abel's head tilts. "Who?"

Zao turns toward Abel, "Someone underground. Obsessed with her field. A geneticist for flora and fauna who has access to DNA records within the Federation's influence."

Abel shrugs. "Great. How do we reach her?"

Zao presses his lips together. "You're not going to like it, but follow me." He swivels his large body and heads to the back storage area. "I recently got involved in another business which connected me to all sorts of characters. One, a doctor who got her start analyzing the DNA of alien animal species but somehow got involved with this guerilla group. Now she fabricates DNA trails, messes up DNA codes to cover their tracks from forensics. Since there's not any legit geneticists coming to Station 17, this woman may be our best shot."

"Sounds like a good place to start."

Zao shuffles through the narrow corridor, his sides occasionally knocking down product. Abel maneuvers around the debris in Zao's wake.

"What group are you talking about?" Abel asks. "And what business?"

Zao doesn't respond. He leads Abel to a much larger room behind the shop. The space is four times the size of the store front, with all sorts of trinkets, gadgets, and artifacts lining the shelves. Treasures from other Collector gigs. Zao glides across the storage room floor, his colorful robes much more vibrant under the room's bright lights and stops at a stack of three olive heavy-duty containers. With a hand on the top one, he turns to face Abel. "Like I said, you're not going to like it." Zao unfastens the latch to one of the containers, and the products inside almost light up Abel's face.

Abel shakes his head, then turns toward Zao. "What the hell?" He rubs his face and lets out a long groan. He gazes back inside the container, filled with military-grade plasma rifles—all lined up in neat order, looking as if they came straight from the factory. Underneath the plasma rifles are energy pistols, as well as what might be explosives. He examines the contents, then turns his attention toward Zao, whose chubby cheeks widen into a large grin.

"What do you say?" Zao emits a mischievous chuckle, "Ever want to arm some terrorists?"

Abel rubs his eyes and shakes his head. "No, can't say the thought has crossed my mind. You sure this is the best way?"

"Best way? No. The only way? Unless you have any expensive warp fuel to jump to another system that may or may not have whom we're looking for. I certainly don't feel like spending thousands of units on—"

"Yeah, I got it." Abel raises his palm. "How is this going to take us to the DNA scrambler?"

"As part of our payment, we can reduce our asking price in exchange for a… consultation, I suppose." Zao shuts the lid and a loud thud rings through the entire storeroom. He heads to the front of the stack of containers and shrugs. "Well? This is my offer. You in or you out? There may be another lead in it for you."

Abel weighs his options. "In my experience, getting involved with radicals usually leads to zero profits and a blaster hole in the chest."

"Look, I know what you're thinking—" Zao takes a step

forward. "Radicals are often unpredictable and trigger-happy. These guys seem solid, and they already gave me an offer on the weapons, of which you can have a small cut and possibly talk to their DNA scrambler."

"How many units are we talking?"

Zao taps a finger on the data pad on his wrist and shows it to Abel.

Seeing the digits on the screen, Abel nods, the gears in his mind shifting.

Zao brightens up like a kid in a candy store. "So—?"

Abel studies the offer on the screen, then meets Zao's stare. "Damn it all, I'd better not get shot."

Zao bursts into excited laughter and smacks his large hand against Abel's shoulder. "Fantastic. The deal is tonight, and don't forget that wretched skull on the counter."

Chapter 5

Art has an ambiguous definition. One cannot simply describe it as brush strokes with oils on canvas. However, the power of it inspires, it speaks, and most of all, it forces us to remember.

These thoughts often run through the man's mind while he browses his collection. Such magnificent art pieces, all collected from every corner of the galaxy. Yet this one intrigues him the most.

It is a huge piece of bloody magnificence. An image of death, decay, pestilence, and darkness. How the greed of the elite forced normal men to fight in a wasteland of disease and mortality. The field ridden with shell casings, rats, gas agents, pieces of uniform and flesh, the closest that Earth has ever physically touched hell.

The man gazes at the oil painted on wood through his slick, ebony metal mask. His breathing muffled by the mask, he wears it not to conceal his identity, but to bring out his true self.

His thoughts trail off. Some would say that true self is that of a monster.

"Keeper?" An angelic, feminine voice interrupts his thoughts. He turns to see a woman wearing a white tailored dress with gold trim on the seams. Her black wavy hair rests on her shoulders. Her green eyes are sharp like spearheads, and her face is sculpted like many of the Greek statues in his collection.

"I imagine you have important news for me, seeing that you have interrupted my intellectual hour." The man's voice is modulated through his mask, often sending chills through the bones of his servants. He stands in a black robe, its hood covering his head as well as his mask.

The woman's chin is lifted as she gives her news. "He has found it."

The man paces toward her with his fingers interlocked behind his back. "Good... good. What of our chosen Buddha?"

The woman shakes her head. "He is making him work for it. As we have expected."

"I see—"

Silence fills the art gallery, lit only by the reflection of a moon through a large glass wall. Yet the light fluctuates; it becomes dark, then bright. The moon appears broken apart, as if Armageddon is a breath away—a visual reminder.

***

The gallery makes the woman uneasy. So many pieces of death and destruction. Depictions of greed, of envy and pride. Not to mention the shattered moon in the sky. She decides to break the silence. "If I may, what is special about him?"

The man's stare pierces into her soul, as if he is counting her heartbeats. "What is special about any of us?"

The woman remains silent, taking in his response.

Interrupting her thoughts, the masked man continues, "Be sure to keep monitoring his progress. Keep me notified of his location and his accomplishments in the investigation." The man turns back to gaze upon the horrific painting, his hazel eyes bright with excitement.

The woman remains as still as water, watching him examine the painting, so intrigued. How strange are men of his status being inspired by hellish events way before their era. Then again, are there other men like him?

"You can go now." His modulated voice booms. She obliges with his wishes. Her heels echo through the gallery and eventually fade out of earshot of the man in the mask. Before the echoes completely disappear, the man calls out to her.

"Cyra?" He calls out with the voice of a commander.

"Yes, Keeper?" She turns immediately, waiting for more inquiries.

"Please notify me when he learns of the identity of the remains."

"As you wish, Keeper." She bows her head and disappears through the gallery exit.

Chapter 6

The sound of industry pollutes the air, even in this abandoned warehouse. Clanking of metal rings through the walls, machinery cuts and mills. Yet the sounds are muffled through the metal walls of the old, empty warehouse. Abel leans against the wall and can almost feel the vibrations from the activities outside.

Cleo hovers idly in the holographic shape of a dog, sitting patiently next to him. Then another sound fills the air, the sound of groaning. Or is it humming?

Abel turns his attention toward the source of the noise with slight annoyance. Zao sits cross-legged on top of the heavy-duty crates containing the energy weapons, humming loudly with his eyes closed.

Abel's teeth grind to Zao's meditating chant, which disrupts the quiet of the entire warehouse. Until he's had enough, then he exclaims, "Must you do that right now?"

Zao pauses his mantra and opens one eye at Abel, sitting perfectly still. "It keeps my mind calm and healthy."

Abel rolls his eyes. "Yeah, you're one to talk about

health. Why do you put on this pose? There aren't many scoundrel concierges out there who meditate and dress like some weird monk."

Zao parts a slight grin and closes his eye. "Says the man who doesn't smoke yet wears a jacket that makes him smell like a tobacco factory." Zao scrunches his nose at the thought and points at Abel's coat. "Where did you get that anyway?"

Abel lets his eyes wander around the warehouse. The recurring dream returns for a moment, then he grumbles, "Some asshole."

"Well... that asshole had class, despite the smell." Zao falls silent. The faint sounds of industry return, as do Cleo's slight hums from her hovering. The whiff of iron and rust permeate the air, along with burning oils and ozone. After a few moments pass, Zao resumes his chants while lying perfectly still.

Abel's annoyance returns as soon as Zao begins his chants and breaks the big man's concentration. "Look, since we're dealing with radicals here, do you mind if I get a piece? For insurance?"

Zao opens both eyes this time. "Ye have no faith in me?"

Abel shakes his head. "Nope. Radicals have faith, but I don't."

With a sigh, Zao rolls off the crates, a slight dent appearing in his wake. Beside the three crates lies a smaller one that they also hauled. Abel tries not to ask too many questions, but he finally gets to see what's inside this crate. Zao kicks the latch open and stands aside. Inside are a dozen handguns in a rack, all constructed of black steel and minor scratches on the surface. The age of the handguns is apparent, but somehow elegant like fine wine.

Zao grips one and lifts it into view, stroking his fat fingers along the slide. "This one here is an oldie but goodie." He says, almost drooling. "The Hudson H9, rechambered for today's common ammunition. The barrel was replaced with a unique metal that magnetizes the projectile, causing increased and more lethal velocity, without punishing your wrist." He offers it to Abel, grinning from ear to ear.

Abel can only stare for a moment, then peers up at Zao. "Really? A slugger?" He takes the pistol and examines it closely, then rubs a finger over one of the scratches. "A few centuries old?"

"Hey, don't knock it till you try it." Zao exclaims while extending his index finger. "These fine pieces are collector items, and they have been modified to fit today's use. It'll suit your needs if the situation calls for *gentle persuasion*."

Abel replies. "Gentle persuasion, huh? And here I thought you said these people were solid."

"They are," Zao says while waddling back to the crates. "Yet, like you said, radicals."

"Hm, right." Abel stuffs the Hudson inside his coat, concealed from sight. "So, who exactly are these people?"

Before Zao can turn around and answer, a loud clang rings throughout the warehouse. Both Abel and Zao straighten and turn toward the clang. Three figures march toward them.

In front is a woman who wears an oil-stained tank top with fatigues tucked into boots. Her body is covered with geometrical tattoos, including one lining the side of her forehead. Her hair is in a loose braid with the sides in a buzzcut. She doesn't seem very tall, but her stance and appearance remain intimidating.

Beside her are two men in jumpsuits, covered in soot and grease. One of them sports a mechanical eye, which glows in sunset orange, like a dim star. The other stands tall and muscular, also covered in tattoos like the woman. His beard is chest length and braided, which seems odd for an industry worker. Then again, their activities tend toward illicit.

"Ah, welcome. Welcome." Zao waddles forward with arms extended, a large grin spreading across his face. The rough trio do not share his enthusiasm. They glare at him until the lead woman speaks up.

"You have something for us?" Her accent sounds very Slavic, which makes Abel guess that she is from the local system.

"Yes, yes." Zao shuffles toward the crates and showcases them, his eyes radiating excitement.

The Sovlikian woman spots Abel with his arms crossed. "We thought it was going to be just you. Who is he?" She demands with a jerk of her head toward Abel. Abel stands stiffly, Cleo next to him, emitting a tiny growl only he can hear.

Zao chuckles nervously, "Oh, he's just muscle. I'm sure you understand."

The woman studies Abel from head to toe, then examines Cleo hovering around him. "Hm. Zao, let's see them."

Zao promptly opens one case to reveal the weaponry inside. Both of the men peer into the case, and grins stretch across their faces. The bearded man picks up a plasma repeater from the case. He toys with the three rotating barrels and pretends to fire the weapon. Zao grins wider with every spin of the barrel.

Suddenly, the man with the beard speaks up, "You got us Typhoons?"

Zao spins toward him. "Why, of course. AR500 Typhoons. For all of your rapid needs." Zao pyramids his fingers and watches the two men examine the weaponry.

After a few minutes, the woman raps on the table. "We'll take them. Same payment as discussed?"

"Not exactly." Abel speaks up, to which Zao and the woman glare at him, as if he were a child interrupting a conversation between two adults. "We'll reduce the price, in exchange for something else."

Zao opens his mouth to shut Abel up but is cut off by the woman whose attention is now on Abel, "Muscle, huh? Okay then, what is this 'something else'?"

Abel clears his throat. "A birdie told me that you have a DNA scrambler serving your cause. I want a consultation."

The woman raises an eyebrow. "We have one, sure. She's an artist, but a valuable asset. Is this why you're here?"

"I have an interesting lead, but I need someone who's good in this field. That's our offer. Reduced price in exchange for a consultation." Abel posts his hands on his hips, waiting for their decision.

The lead woman glances at the other two men, who both shrug. Then she turns back to Abel and Zao. "Seems like a fair deal. We need these weapons and we trust Zao, so a consultation you shall have."

Abel peers at Zao, and Zao returns a shrug. Abel looks back at the woman. "Well, that seemed easier than I thought."

"It is simple. You betray us, and we slaughter you where you stand," The woman replies with an ice-cold tone.

"Ah, I wouldn't have it any other way." Abel says with a slight groan. "When can we see her?"

"As soon as we close this deal. I want to have my people armed as soon as possible." The woman strides over to the crates and runs her fingers across the cold aluminum of the weaponry.

"Who are your people, exactly?" Abel asks.

The Sovlikian woman glances up at him. "I'm sure you've heard of us?" Her eyes scan the room, then answers just above a whisper. "We're the Satyr Militia."

"Ah." Abel nods. "So those eco-terrorists on the news."

"Eco-warriors," the man with the mechanical eye exclaims from behind the woman. "The Federation believes they are the masters of these new worlds, but we aim to show them different."

"It's okay. We're not fond of you either." The woman states. "Collectors have been known to destroy entire mountains and disrupt wildlife just to get to artifacts. Which I've gathered that is your profession."

"Of a sort," Abel replies. "I don't exactly excavate the planets for ruins, just small artifacts."

"I see that your recent expedition has showed you that those worlds bite back," The woman motions toward his blister scars.

"Beats a desk job," Abel says a bit louder. "So does that change your mind about me seeing your DNA scrambler?"

The Sovlikian woman smirks, then barks at the two men. "Sergei. Vadim. Load the crates onto the hauler. We're bringing our new associates with us."

The bearded man, whom Abel presumes is Sergei, shouts, "Will do, Natasha. We'll be in the air in no time."

Natasha turns back toward Abel, Zao, and Cleo. "Well?

Let's get going. Our DNA scrambler is a busy girl and she's about to get even more so."

"Wait, I'm going too?" Zao asks with an exasperated frown.

Abel slaps his hand on Zao's back and smirks, "Don't worry. big guy, I'm sure there's a noodle bowl for your efforts."

Zao lets out a soft sigh and peers up at Abel. "The cost of fortune, am I right?"

Abel smiles. "The cost of fortune."

Chapter 7

The cost of fortune.

The words whisper back to Abel's mind. He sits on a log by a roaring campfire, while other young Collectors sit alongside him, all listening with intent, curiosity and excitement. Their eyes focus on the old man, bald with a longer gray beard. Despite the intense aroma of synthesized tobacco, the man dresses with rugged class and stands with the posture of a nobleman.

Ser Kodak, always the gentleman adventurer.

They listen to him, soaking up his teachings of the Collector life. He paces around them like a motivational speaker delivering his product. Yet for young Abel, Ser Kodak is his messiah.

"Remember, lads and lasses, the journeys ahead of you will be tests of your will. You will hurt, you will break, and sometimes you won't even savor the sweet taste of an award. For every lead is a gamble, and a gamble with high stakes.

"However, every single one of you come from broken homes. Ravaged colonies, the result of a war that nobody will win. Places of struggle where, if I haven't found you, none of you would have been able to escape. Orphans, victims of abuse, slaves to a society driven by status. A gamble is usually the best odds that you have ever known."

Ser Kodak takes a long puff of his cigar, then continues. "Remember that the true measure of your greatness in the eyes of those scums of the Federation are wealth and memories. Wealth for power, and memories for influence. Both of which you will achieve in this life. If you are smart and if you listen to me. Some of you will break, and some of you may even die."

His words fall upon the group. Abel looks over at Ethan, whose mouth hangs open at Ser Kodak's speech.

"For that, my apprentices, is the cost of fortune."

Abel takes in those words for the thousandth time, and once again he hears the whispers in the wind, the all-familiar soft voice.

Wake up.

Abel wakes with sudden gasps, this time in the backseat of a hauler, cruising above the surface between skyscrapers of Station 17. Natasha is startled by Abel's sudden awakening, and she sneers in response.

"Bad dream?" She asks.

"He does that every now and then." Zao speaks up from beside her.

The two Satyr Militia men are in the front two seats of the hauler, navigating the labyrinth that is Station 17. Natasha and Zao sit in the back with Abel, and Cleo is nested in his messenger bag.

"We're arriving at the compound," Vadim announces from the driver's seat.

"Good. Please notify the welcome party ahead of time

that we have two passengers," Natasha calls out from the backseat. "Also, please notify Dr. Morgan that she will have guests."

"Will do." Vadim nods.

"Let's get one thing straight," Natasha now speaks to both Zao and Abel, her fingers splayed in a no-nonsense fashion. "This is our compound. You do what I say. Any sudden moves, any signs that you're working for the Federation, and we turn you both into beef mince. Understand?"

Abel and Zao both nod and mutter an answer.

"Good." Natasha leans back. "Dr. Morgan is our DNA scrambler, although she is a little scrambled herself. But she should be able to help you."

"Wait, scrambled how?" Zao asks.

"Oh, she hears voices and is a little skittish, but geniuses are never perfect," Natasha answers while Abel and Zao exchange glances.

Finally, Sergei speaks up from the front of the ship, "We're docking now."

Abel and Zao gasp. The ship seems to be flying into the side of one of the skyscrapers. Yet, a second before they collide with the structure, the building opens, revealing a lit tunnel leading deep into the heart of the building. The ship slows, and the cabin begins to rattle while the ship brakes for landing. It hovers over the landing pad, as Vadim slowly sets the hauler down for the landing gear to kiss the surface. Finally, the ship shakes with a hard thud, and the landing pad rotates the ship to face toward the exit for future takeoff.

Everyone unbuckles their seatbelts to make their way out of the ship. As Abel and Zao head down the boarding ramp, they are greeted by a group of rugged, armed militants. They stand at varying heights and wear uniforms representing different industries and manufacturing plants. Every member has their own unique traits, whether man or woman, and each sports unique braids and tattoos. One even seems to be a reprogramed industry bot, standing tall over its human colleagues.

They eye Abel, but focus more on the old man with his colored robes, piercing him with suspicious glimpses. Abel spots some of the militants white-knuckling the grips of their weapons. Despite the different genders and races, the militants and the Federation marines have the same attitude. They are waiting for an excuse to spill blood.

"We need some of you unload the cargo." Natasha barks at the group of militants, who straighten their posture in response. "Sergei, please escort Abel and Zao to Dr. Morgan's lab."

Sergei nods, then Natasha pivots toward Abel and Zao. "I have business to attend to. Remember, we're all watching you." She whirls around and marches out with two militants in escort.

Sergei motions at Abel and Zao. "Follow me." He marches into the compound. Abel follows, with Zao struggling to keep the brisk pace.

Inside the compound, squads of militants patrol the corridors, exchanging looks at their new visitors. Their suspicious glances make Abel nervous. They're in the heart of it, amid a scores of militants dedicated to fighting authority.

Sergei stops before a metallic door. "Here we are. Remember, I will be waiting out here in case you two try anything." He stands off to the side with his arms crossed, a slight snarl in his lip.

Abel presses the controls on the side, and the doors slide open with a soft hiss. Zao follows him as he steps inside, and the both of them gasp at the same time.

Chaos. The lab is a cluttered mess. Lab equipment is set on the counters in a disorganized fashion with vials and scanners scatter around. DNA codes and gibberish line the walls. Books--actual printed tomes—line the wall shelves.

"I thought my shop was cluttered." Zao mumbles, trying not to knock over any lab equipment.

A woman peeks from behind one of the lab counters and gives Abel and Zao a startle. She examines them over large spectacles as she crouches over her lab equipment. Silence fills the void between them.

"Uh—" Abel breaks the silence. "You must be Dr. Morgan?"

"Eva Morgan. Call me Eva," She replies, her voice soft like a whisper. Her auburn hair is frizzled and in need of a wash. Her face is plain, but the brown eyes behind her spectacles are wide with wonder, almost as if she doesn't blink. Her body is sparrow-like, and when she stands, she's shorter than Zao. A ragged lab coat covers her fatigues, and her fingernails show signs of biting.

Abel and Zao exchange glimpses. Scrambled is an understatement. Abel turns to Eva. "We were hoping you could—"

"You carry the dead with you?" Eva interrupts him.

Abel is taken back by her quick assumption. "I'm sorry?"

Eva vaults over the counter and refers to his messenger bag. "The remains. I can smell them."

Zao takes a few steps backward and Abel replies, "How can you—? It doesn't matter." He removes the container from his bag and shows it to Eva. She takes it out of his hands with great care and opens the lid.

The skull stares back with its hollow eyes. Yet, rather than surprised by the remains, Eva appears intrigued. As if those hollow eyes belong to an old friend.

"We are hoping you can help us find the identity of this person," Abel says. "Found it close to a *Starglider* wreckage on a planet not yet touched by humans."

Eva sets it on the counter and examines it closely. "Poor soul. Alone…frightened." She then hovers her finger over the bullet hole. "Betrayed—"

Abel then looks back at Zao, who shrugs and stands a few paces behind him, as if Eva will pounce on him.

Eva spins around to face Abel. "I can help you, but I need time to speak with it."

"Wait, speak?" Abel leans in. Did he hear her right? Eva holds the container close to her chest.

"A few hours, then we shall know." Eva's voice doesn't seem to be Sovlikian or the standard dialect of the Federation. Why is she here? Eva doesn't fit in with the rest of the group here, and Abel is losing faith in her the longer he stands in this lab. But he's intrigued by her handling of the skull, and her demeanor is not threatening, though strange. He decides to trust her. "Okay. What should we do in the meantime?" Abel asks while twisting to gaze around the lab.

"Stay." She replies softly. "Perhaps you can provide insight." Eva darts out the laboratory door, and through the window, he can see her exchanging a few words with Sergei outside the door, to which he gives an affirming nod. She returns to her lab and begins her work on one of the instruments.

"There's coffee and snacks around the corner." She waves her hand toward the corner of the lab, showing a flimsy snack cart with opened wrappers scattered around the floor.

The next few hours are quiet, besides the clanking of glassware and lab equipment. Eva works frantically, examining the skull and jumping back and forth from the equipment to the data monitor. Zao tries to meditate to pass the time, but the disorganization of the lab causes him to pace. Abel sits reclined while monitoring possible leads and market research on Starskin scrap. Cleo displays this data in front of him while posing as a hawk.

Finally, Eva hovers over the counter, muttering to herself, her eyes glued to the data monitor. Her sudden break in behavior has caused Abel to notice and he rises from the chair.

"You've figured out who the mysterious wonder is?" Abel asks moving closer. Zao's attention is also now focused on Eva, his fingers forming into a pyramid.

Eva shifts to face Abel, staring at him as if she has seen a ghost. "Impossible—"

Abel tilts his head. "What is it?"

Eva takes off her spectacles. "Does this skull seem familiar to you? Is that why you brought it?"

Abel is taken back by the question and sets his hands on his hips. "I found it on a place where no human has been before, allegedly, and there is that bullet hole. My curiosity got the best of me."

A few moments of silence fill the void in the room, and Eva picks at her nails, then turns to him. "This skull knows you."

"Huh?" Abel says.

Eva carefully picks up the skull and holds it in front of her chest, pointing its hollow eyes toward Abel, then whispers, "It is you."

Chapter 8

The words sink like a rock in water. They whisper in his mind, compromising his grasp on reality. *It is you. It is you. It is you.*

His vision tunnels, his heartbeat races, and his eyes stare into the hollow, dark pits of the eyeholes of the human skull. Again, he senses that odd feeling he's had ever since he picked it up off Aegis 12, perhaps the feeling that enticed him to take it in the first place.

Familiarity.

Zao's laughter makes Abel snap out of his trance. "That's ridiculous. He's standing right here. This is a waste of time, a crazy woman telling ghost stories."

"No stories," she replies, her eyes narrowing at the large man. Eva steps out of the way for them to view the monitor. Sure enough, she has cross-referenced the DNA results of the remains with the Federation DNA citizen registry. The list shows multiple checks, a 100-percent match to one citizen. Abel.

The confirmation sends Abel's mind spiraling. Perhaps this woman has been hatching this fabrication to deceive them. Or she's covering up for whomever this skull may actually belong to. But why? Abel studies the woman. He's only just met her, but for some reason, he trusts her. Her mentality, her fervor, the way she speaks to the remains as if it still has a soul—this is not a woman who lies.

Abel turns to Zao, who's discussing the possibilities why the results came to be. He suggests the works could be the result of another DNA scrambler. Yet Eva replies that the sample is completely original. Abel only hears whispers and muffled voices.

He studies Zao. A scoundrel, a man who has cheated for a few units, a known liar. He may have helped Abel, but there's always something in it for him. Maybe someone else came along. As he watches him argue with Eva, the corners of the lab seem to whisper conspiracy.

Abel snatches a nearby syringe and grabs Zao by the throat. Despite his heavy weight, Abel pins him against the wall with the sheer combined force of anger and paranoia and presses the tip of the syringe against his neck. Zao's eyes are ripe with fear.

"What game are you playing?" Abel demands with a cold whisper.

Zao stutters, "N-n no game. You know—"

"Bullshit." Abel presses the syringe into his neck. Zao gasps. Eva backs up, gnawing on a fingernail, seemingly unfazed by what's happening in front of her. "You sent me on a lead where I find my own body. What the hell is this?"

"I don't know," Zao whimpers. "Abel, buddy, please be reasona—"

"I am reasonable," Abel's voice booms. Sergei charges into the lab, but stops confused at what he sees.

"If you don't tell me, then I am taking an eye." Abel

inches the syringe up, touching its tip to his lid. In that moment, a flash appears in his mind.

The flash is sudden, yet the feeling is real. Cold, metallic bonds compress his wrist. The sudden feeling of fear, helplessness, and loneliness envelops him. A jolt causes him to startle back and drop the syringe. A row of lights surround him, and a needle comes close to his eye.

He falls back, and Zao catches his breath. Abel leans against the lab counter, his breath failing him. "Wha... what?"

"Are you insane?" Zao's face is red hot. "I have no idea how your own skull was on that wretched planet, but I am not out to get you."

Abel supports himself on the counter and stands. "What is going on?" he whispers to himself.

The lab suddenly shakes, and glassware falls off the counters and shatters to the ground. The compound roars like an earthquake, then a series of plasma fire, shouting, and screams plague the air.

The sounds of war echo from the halls.

Natasha bursts into the lab, covered in soot, a gash bleeding on her head. "I hope you got what you're looking for because we need to go now."

"What's going on?" Zao asks.

Natasha's breathing comes in spurts. "We've been compromised. Federation marines have breached our compound and we're already losing ground. Somebody betrayed us." She aims a slugger at Zao's forehead, switching between Zao and Abel. In response, Zao raises his hands , but Abel remains focused on the startling discovery.

"What did I tell you about betraying us?" Natasha growls.

Her tone quickly changes when a gun presses to her temple. Sergei releases a large grin as he presses the plasma pistol hard into Natasha's head. "You have too much faith," he says, his accent thick.

Her slugger remains steady, and her body still. Zao and Abel freeze. Out of the corner of his eye, Abel glimpses Eva hiding behind one of the lab counters.

"Why, Sergei?" Natasha whimpers. "Why do this to everything we have built?"

Sergei's grin fades. "After years of fighting, I have seen many friends die. Many worlds conquered by those we fight. We fight to the death, yet the enemy presses on as if we were mere tics," Sergei babbles, justifying his betrayal. Meanwhile, Zao leans over to whisper to Abel.

"This is not our fight, but we're in the middle of it. We need to find a way out."

"Agreed," Abel replies, managing to find his voice again. "Many of these people are going to get slaughtered, as we will, if we don't get past these two."

Abel and Zao begin whispering a plan, until Natasha suddenly turns toward Sergei and fires into him point blank. Her weapon flashes and emits a loud boom, which muffles Sergei's sudden cries of pain. Blood splatters on the wall behind him and he stumbles back. In a flash, he returns fire and Natasha's cries of pain ring through the lab. They exchange shots. In seconds, they both fall against the walls.

Abel and Zao stand there, mouths open. Sergei lets out a chuckle. His eyes widen. He coughs. A gush of blood gurgles from his mouth. "So much for my fortune—" His eyes roll back. Lifeless eyes.

Natasha leans against the wall, her hands desperately

trying to staunch the flow of blood gushing from her throat. Her boots slip on the puddle of blood forming around her. Death gurgles her last breaths. The gurgling stops, and her hands drop.

Abel glances at Zao, then spots Eva with her hands over her ears, rocking back and forth by the counter.

"Well, what the hell?" Zao exclaims.

"That's one less obstacle," Abel says, then strides toward Sergei's corpse to pick up his weapon, trying not to slip on the blood.

"Listen, this whole station is going to be on lockdown, since this seems to be a raid to wipe these guys out." He checks his weapon, and a small charging noise emits from the plasma pistol. "My ship is still in the hangars. If we can get there fast enough, we may escape before they close the ports."

Zao sighs and rubs his temples. "This is insane. We can just wait this out in my shop."

"They'll be looking for us," Eva announces from behind the counter. "Like dogs on the hunt, they'll sniff out any wrongdoers."

"Especially you." Zao points to Eva. "You say this as if you're coming with us."

"She is," Abel says. "I still need her for this little mystery."

Zao smirks. "You can't be serious. This is your biggest concern?"

"My concern is to get off this station, and you're coming with me too." Abel moves toward Zao, his weapon in hand. "I still have questions. Plenty of them. And you're going to answer all of them."

Zao visibly gulps. They stare at each other in silence, the

sound of explosions and screams erupting from the corridors. "If we—"

"When we get off this station," Abel cuts Zao off. Cleo approaches Abel, and he turns his attention to the holographic hawk. "Cleo, they're about to close the ports, so I need you to work your magic. Scramble flight records, get us off the no-fly list, mess with their flight schedules—whatever you gotta do. Meet us back at *The Tip of the Spear* for takeoff. You'll know when."

The hawk beeps in confirmation, then takes flight through the lab door, simulating a majestic hawk flying through the chaos.

Eva watches in awe as Cleo takes off. Abel turns toward Zao and Eva with his new pistol pointed in the air. "Are you two ready?"

They both nod. He then grabs the container holding the skull and shuts it tight, and stuffs it in his messenger bag. "Good, stay close to me."

The newly formed trio open the lab doors, and the brutal conflict becomes reality. Corpses of Satyr militants litter the halls, as well as some marines. To the right of the doors, militants return fire, taking cover by the doorways lining the halls. Marines shoot from cover at the end of the hallway, their voices modulated through their helmets so the enemy cannot hear them communicate.

One militant peeks from cover to fire, and a burst of red mist explodes from the back of one marine and falls to the ground. The marine's squad mate returns fire, and a splash of blood explodes from the militant's side. His arm flies off, causing his weapon to drop to the ground. The militant's companion pulls him back to cover, and Abel frantically looks for a way out. Eva darts to the left, running from cover to cover down the hallway.

"Where is she going?!" Zao screams over the chaos.

Abel turns to him. "To the exit. Come on." He darts off, Zao on his heels. Despite Zao's bright robes and large size, he manages to dash from one cover to another without getting shot. Abel follows Eva's tracks and focuses on a speedy retreat. Eva effortlessly maneuvers through the cover and corpses, avoiding the chaos of plasma fire and militants rushing past them to join the firefight.

Finally, they reach a peaceful hall, as more Satyr militants rush pass them. Zao is the last to catch up, wiping blood off his eyes. "Wha…that man's head just…Oh, sweet mercy." He says and swipes at his face.

Abel pivots toward Eva, his breath coming in spurts. "I assume you know the way out?"

Eva nods and slams the door controls behind her. Before them sits a laundry room as dim as murky water. Eva wastes no time and dashes in. Abel and Zao quickly follow.

Controls litter the room along with baskets of sheets and clothes. Eva runs over to a latch on the wall, which opens a dark chute to the lower floors.

"This way," she says and struggles to climb through.

"Hold on." Abel rests a hand on her shoulder and pulls her away from the chute. Then he turns toward Zao. "You first."

"Why?" The stress of conflict and death is becoming more apparent in his voice.

"Because I don't want you falling on my head at the bottom. So come on." Abel waves his hand to the shoot.

Zao lets out a groan. "Fine." He attempts to climb into the chute. His legs struggle against his weight. Finally, Eva and Abel give him a shove, and his body disappears down the chute, his screams echoing all the way.

Eva then climbs in and slides down with no sound. Abel follows, and he finds himself in total darkness. The chute is drafty, and the metallic surface feels like ice against his skin. For a few exhilarating seconds, they slide like teenagers in a park until they fall into a large bin full of linens.

The three of them lay there for a moment. Abel enjoys the comfort and quiet of the sheets. The firefight inside the compound resounds beyond the walls, and muffled sirens ring from outside the station. The trio climb out of the bin and scout the laundry building of the lower floors of the compound. Their search leads to an attached but separate building, with no marines in sight.

The three catch their breaths, then analyze their surroundings. The sounds of the firefight echo from the compound, yet now sounds of life come from outside the building. Normal sounds reach their ears—the buzz of industry going about its business and the chatter of crowds gathering outside the compound. A Federation announcement booms from outside, telling passing citizens to move on, that this is state business.

"Come on." Abel darts for the exit, and Eva and Zao follow him. Abel presses the open key, and the doors slide open to the commotion of crowds outside. News drones circle around the compound to try to catch images of the firefight.

"I'm never arms dealing again." Zao mumbles to himself as he waddles through the crowds.

"We need to take to the stars," Eva says.

"I'm working on it," Abel says over his shoulder as he weaves through the crowds. "Just keep following me. We have to make it to the hangars."

Anxiety is creeping back into Abel's mind. The crowds and the lights of the news drones make his heart pace faster. He can't stop thinking about the new discovery. His skull, on Aegis 12? How is it even possible? Also, what was the flash he saw before he threatened Zao with the syringe to his eye? Was it an illusion, a memory? Has he lost his mind?

Finally, they find their way to the metro system and wait for a train. After a few moments, a train comes whirring into the stop, and the doors open with a soft hiss. The trio hurry onto the train, trying to look as inconspicuous as possible. They make an odd sight—a rugged man holding a pistol, a portly monk rubbing blood off his face with his robes, and a twitchy doctor batting at an imagined fly.

Abel receives a pop-up alert on his data pad, stating that *The Tip of the Spear* was transferred to a private hangar free from the sealed ports. Also included are the location of the hangar and the scheduled takeoff time. *Oh Cleo, where would he be without her?*

"Listen up." Abel leans in to whisper to Zao and Eva. "Cleo managed to get the ship transferred to a private hangar. It seems the Federation is too busy to notice. We gotta get off at that stop Cleo mentioned."

"Wait, what about resupply?" Zao whispers. "I doubt you have enough E.V.A. suits on the ship, let alone my size. Also, there's food, water, etc. And do you even have enough room for us?"

"I'll figure something out." Abel ponders this information. In fact, he has absolutely no E.V.A. suits, since his got sliced up due to his medical emergency on Aegis 12. Not to mention he needs a refuel for the ship. Whatever their errands may be, they'd have to exit at the next closest stop to buy them some time.

"We're going to Loberon," Abel whispers to the other two. "It's the closest stop and we can enter the atmosphere once we leave the station."

Zao frowns, while Eva seems to be trying to catch an invisible butterfly fluttering in the air behind him. "Okay, that could work," Zao says. "There are oil settlements on Loberon. We can stop at one on the farthest hemisphere away from the station."

"Sounds like a plan." Abel says, digesting this new information. The key will be reaching the hangar before the firefight at the compound ends. That will give them enough time to take off without questions asked.

The train begins to slow as all the standing passengers slightly lean forward. The doors slide open, and citizens begin pouring out.

"We can hop off here," Abel states. "Let's go."

Chapter 9

The next half hour becomes a blur.

The trio find the hangar and are cleared for takeoff. *The Tip of the Spear* is still in the same shape as Abel left it.

Eva seems awed at the interior, running her hand over the chromatic plating. Cleo sits by the open boarding ramp in the shape of a hound, as if waiting for her master.

The party boards the ship and hurries to attach their seatbelts. Abel hastily starts his flight check as Zao struggles to fit into the co-pilot's seat.

Eva takes a seat by the engineering panel and gazes into the screen, its blue light highlighting her face.

The Tip of the Spear was originally meant for a crew of four—a pilot, co-pilot, navigator and engineer. Thanks to Cleo, Abel has been able to operate it with just him and the A.I. Yet this time, he has actual bodies filling the seats. Despite how odd they may be, he feels a sense of relief.

"All right, we're taking off, initiating thrusters." Abel announces, and the ship's engines begin to whir. Almost as soon as they begin, the engines roar with dragon fire. The entire ship shakes and begins to hover off the landing pad.

Zao and Eva grip the armrests of their seats while Abel maneuvers the ship to the stars. Slowly, passing lights flash the cockpit. Then the hangar doors open above them, and the vast, star-lit space comes into view, along with the lights from Station 17.

The ship turns, and thrusts forward. They fly along the skyscraper skyline, gazing at the tall towers of the large space station. Amazing, even for a system as far as this from the center of the Federation's influence, they were able to construct something this colossal.

"All right. Loberon, here we come." Abel manipulates the controls and tilts the ship toward the face of the planet below.

From the vastness of space, Loberon shows tints of grey, blue, and titanium white, displaying an icy wasteland. Fleets of ships transfer from Loberon and Station 17, and occasionally ships jump to other planets and systems in a brilliant flash of light.

Soon, the planet becomes larger in view, and the ship rumbles as fire engulfs it in a magnificent display.

"We're entering the atmosphere. Everyone hang on tight," Abel announces. Zao clenches the arms of his seat as Eva giggles.

"Like angels," she says with a wide smile.

Zao peers back at her. "First time landing on a planet?"

She shouts, "First time on a ship."

The Tip of the Spear rumbles and shakes with the fury of a god until finally the fire retracts, and their field of view becomes clouded. Water droplets coat the glass of the cockpit until they break through the clouds. Before them lies a mountainous tundra. The droplets freeze on the glass.

Ice and snow sheets the surface of Loberon, and the air

is strangely calm for their descent. Abel flies the ship low between the mountains, and the snow blows off the ground as the ship passes.

"Zao, where are we headed?" Abel speaks over his shoulder at Zao, who plays with the monitor.

"Uh, let's see. There's a small oil-trading post not far from this valley. Start heading west."

"Perfect." Abel turns the controls and loops around a jagged mountain.

After a few moments of surfing the air, a small outpost appears in the distance. From a grouping of miniscule structures, a few ships come and go on their landing pads. Some ships even land outside the outpost if no landing pad is available.

"There's no traffic control here, so just find a spot," Zao says when the trading post comes closer into view.

"Ah fairly relaxed, my kind of place," Abel says with a small grin.

Luckily, as they approach, a ship takes off from a landing pad. Abel manipulates the ship onto the free landing pad. With a light thud, the ship lands and slows to a stop.

They unclick their seatbelts and lift themselves out of their seats, then head for the center hub of the ship until Abel holds up a hand. "Wait, everyone."

Eva and Zao stop in their tracks.

"Like I said, I have questions," Abel says and focuses on Zao. "Now that we have a breather."

Zao sighs and steps forward. "Fair enough. Ask away."

Chapter 10

The hub of the ship is as silent as whispers. Zao stands waiting for Abel to ask his questions, while Eva takes a seat at the center table and chews on her thumb nail.

Abel clears his throat. "Who gave you the lead to Aegis 12?"

Zao sighs. "Abel, you know I can't give—" He stops for a moment, then continues, "A woman."

"What woman?" Abel crosses his arms and glares at Zao.

Zao shrugs. "I don't know. She wore a hood. Judging by her clothes, she was high class."

"High class? Did she come to you?"

"Yes. She came into the shop one day. The woman somehow found out about my... activities and suggested this lead on Aegis 12."

"Why would she do that?" Abel asks, his head tilting.

"The woman said she was a Collector herself, but this time she couldn't risk being on the planet." Zao mopped his forehead. "Her main objective was to find out what was on it, and she didn't expect to take a cut of the profits."

"Any reason why she would want to know what was there? And how did she even know about the *Star Glider* wreckage?"

"She said she detected an anomaly on the surface. I'm guessing the woman didn't know what was there. Then again she didn't say much." Zao paces around the hub.

Abel grabs his flimsy camping chair and unfolds it. He sits down and kicks his feet up on the center table, causing Eva to flinch and scoot over. "This doesn't make sense. Why would another Collector not share in any cut or profits from the dig?"

Zao shrugs again. "I don't know. She didn't seem like the typical Collector."

Abel groans. "That's because she's not a Collector, Zao. The high-class clothes, the anonymity. That can't be a coincidence."

"I agree." Zao stops pacing. "She didn't request you specifically, which is odd—"

Abel bites his lip. "How lucrative did she say the site would be?"

Zao's eyes light up. "She said it should be highly lucrative based on her scans."

"And what did you say to me when I walked into your shop?"

Zao thinks, then sighs. "That you were my favorite, and you get dibs on the good gigs."

"Exactly." Abel shoots to his feet. "She must've known that you were going to give me the lead first. She may be someone we know from the past or someone who's watching us closely."

"But why?" Zao frowns. "What does she want to do with some treasure hunters?"

"We should ask her," Abel says. "Any idea where she may be?"

"Let me think." Zao rubs his temples. "She said that if there were any interesting developments, such as the Collector finding anything substantial, she usually spends nights gazing at art under Armageddon."

Abel tilts his head back. "What the hell does that mean?"

"I don't know." Zao leans his heavy hands on the center table. "Assuming she was hoping for you to find whatever was there, then maybe you have an idea?"

"Not the slightest." Abel exhales. *How is any of this possible? Finding his own remains on a distant and toxic planet.* He turns toward Eva, who's staring at the wall. "Eva."

Her wide eyes dart toward him.

"My skull. Being found on another planet. How is that even possible?"

She pauses, her eyes flitting around the room. "The universe is flexible like rubber. There are rules, yet the universe is tangible."

Abel's brows furrow. She mutters nonsense, yet anything crazy seems normal at this point.

"Could be time, engineering, the fabric of reality slipping," she continues.

"Have you ever been cloned or duplicated?" Zao asks.

Abel is taken back by the question. "No, I still remember my youth and my past. I don't remember waking up in a lab."

"Memories can be funny." She shifts to look at him. "They are fragile. But cloning is not the answer. DNA would be slightly different."

"Well, it looks like it could be several possibilities."

Abel says leaning against the wall. "Obviously, the next step is to find that woman."

"The next step is rest, resupply, and refuel." Zao chimes, his fingers listing their needs. "We can't just keep pressing on like this, and we don't even know if the Federation knows that we were in that firefight at the Satyr Militia's compound."

"Rest refuels the mind," Eva whispers.

Zao pays no attention to her. He sets his hands on Abel's shoulders. "I know this is all a shock to you, and I'm sorry for sending you to Aegis 12. We may not exactly be best friends, but I respect you as a Collector."

Abel freezes in place, uncomfortable with the hand on his shoulder.

"But you need to slow down. We will find that woman and solve this little mystery." Zao finally steps away.

Abel nods slowly. Zao is right. He needs rest. With everything slowing down momentarily, exhaustion envelops his body. His arms are heavy, his eyelids long to close, and his legs ache.

"All right," He says to the two of them. "We should probably scout out the trading post to see what supplies we can get."

"There you go." Zao shuffles toward the bay area of the ship. "We'll take care of our needs, and then we can get on with this puzzle." He stops by the door and spins around. "Oh, we're also going to need to get some warm weather gear. It's cold outside after all."

Abel wanders toward the bay area of the ship. "I suppose I can use a walk around town. I'll see what I can scrounge up."

"Good idea," Zao says. "I'll stay with…uh…looney

here."

Eva shoots Zao a crazed look, which brings a grin.

Abel chuckles softly and opens the boarding ramp of the ship. "Try not to have too much fun." He marches outside.

The bite of winter immediately greets Abel's face. The winds are moderate, yet intense enough to be noticeable. Abel sees his breath when he exhales, and the cool air almost refreshes his body as he inhales. Snow crunches under his boots.

The outpost in front of him is small but busy, ships coming and going. A couple dozen structures form this outpost along with satellite dishes, solar panels, and workers performing their duties. Abel stands watching two workers unload cargo from a ship and a technician refueling one at a landing pad. Small fuel vehicles pass each other between landing pads. A small drone roams around in the cold air, sparks flying as it works.

The scene reminds Abel of his old home. The colony he grew up in during his youth was slightly larger than this trading post on Loberon, yet the atmosphere was the same. Those small outposts and colonies suppress the ambitions of the youth. Abel was always a big dreamer, but his family often suppressed his dreams with the harsh realities of life. That money and security were the most important goals in life, the only ambitions worth having.

Yet he sees the trading post occupants. How hard they work, how worn their faces are, how grim their circumstances. "Settling down" seems quite the opposite. If it weren't for good ole Ser Kodak, he would've been like those people, trapped in a snowy village. He wanders between the structures of this outpost. Shop signs and service stations glow with neon lights through the bitter air.

Perhaps it isn't so bad here. The Collector life is exciting. He has made more money than he would in several lifetimes on an outpost like this, and he has seen beautiful and terrible places. He has witnessed alien wildlife, peaceful as well as aggressive.

Despite his exciting life, he's reminded of his mortality by the skull on a radioactive wasteland. What are the odds? Part of him doesn't want to know the end of this road, and the other part wants to stay here and hide from the truth. Perhaps settle down, work a simple job and bury that skull somewhere out in the deep snow.

Despite his urges, he buries those feelings deep. Deeper than the snow and ice, he'll bury the skull in his mind. Once again, his curiosity overcomes his reserve. *I have to do this. I owe it to myself to find who did this. Who killed me?*

That is another cause of concern. Who would kill him? Plenty of enemies from the past. One can't make a fortune and live the lifestyle he does without making a few. Yet, enough to follow him to a radioactive wasteland and blast him in the head? No one hates him that much.

Abel spots a small shop with winter and adventure gear. He greets the clerk and finds a large winter coat for Zao and a smaller frame coat for Eva, both made of insulating materials.

He wanders back to the ship and climbs the boarding ramp. Appreciating the warmth, he heads into the center hub with the coats slung over his arm.

Zao sits on the center table in his meditating position, humming softly. Eva scratches DNA strains on the walls of the ship while Cleo hovers close to her shoulder in the shape of a hawk again.

"C'mon, Eva." Abel whines.

Eva spins around at his words.

"Just not on the walls, please." Abel sets the coats down next to Zao, who opens one eye and pauses his humming. "There," Abel grumbles, then stifles a yawn. "I'm going to bed."

"Goodnight, sweetheart." Zao replies.

"Right." Abel wanders into his quarters like a walking corpse. The all-familiar cot calls to him, seducing him into sleep. Without changing out of his clothes, he lies on his back, feeling his body sink into the cot. Soon enough, he drifts into the sweet darkness of sleep.

Familiarity returns to his nostrils with the sweet smell of the crisp air. The lights dancing in the sky return to his view as he awakens on the damp soil. He lifts his torso up off the ground and peers around. The Collector Camp.

Young Collectors wander around the camp performing different duties. The beauty of Promethium is more apparent with the sunrise, and the liveliness of the camp gives Abel a comfortable feeling.

In the midst of his thoughts, somebody taps his shoulder. Ethan gawks down on him.

"C'mon, big man says he wants us for an assignment," Ethan says with a tired voice.

Ethan wanders toward a small gathering by the edge of the grassy cliffside. Abel follows him, the cool grass and soft soil feeling like cushions underneath his feet.

"All right, lads and lasses," Ser Kodak's voice falls upon the group of young Collectors. "We have a fix on the site in the caverns northeast of here. You five are my selected scouts."

Abel and Ethan exchange glances as the other Collectors whisper to each other. Ser Kodak continues. "The complication is that *The Tip of the Spear* is out of commission. The other ships are out as well, so you five will travel by foot. It should be a two-day journey."

Ser Kodak reeks of synthesized tobacco more than usual this morning. He puffs his cigar between each sentence, a sign of stress, which could be due to the ships being out of commission.

Or perhaps this gig is the real deal.

Ser Kodak waves his hand at thin air. Then he coughs. "Cleo, please come over here."

From a distant container, a sphere resting on top lights up with life. It hovers off the dented metal, forms a holographic hawk body, and flaps its wings to join the group.

"Now, this here is Cleo," Ser Kodak exclaims. "She was a project that I've been working on for a while. She will lead you to the potential site and act as a reference data base for culture, geography, and fauna and flora." Ser Kodak takes another puff. "I also added the feature for her to take the shape of various earth animals long extinct. Just a little touch to add personality to the little bugger."

Cleo beeps in response, and the group of Collectors, including Abel, stand in awe.

"Now, Cleo will guide you. Don't damage her. If you do, your ass will be on a spike," Kodak warns the group with a grainy voice. "Now gear up and get to it."

Abel breaks from the group to go pack his gear. Ethan joins him.

"Extinct animals from Earth? That's a little ghostly, ain't it?" Ethan says.

Abel lets out a sigh and mutters back, "The big man has a way with dramatic details. He's a big history buff."

"Have you ever been to Earth?" Ethan asks.

Abel shoots him a sour look. "Does it look like I've been to Earth? I spent my whole life on a shitty colony that nobody cares about."

Ethan stops and rests a hand on his shoulder, which Abel promptly swats away. "Why are you being an asshole?" Ethan asks, hands posted on his waist.

Abel sighs, his body slouched. He replies, "Look, buddy. I'm not here to make friends. Unlike you, this isn't a field trip to me. I'm here to make a fortune, like most of these sorry lots." He turns around and stalks off, with Ethan on his heels.

"That's what matters, isn't it?"

"Yep," Abel says. He reaches the campsite and finds his gear. As he is stuffing his bag, Ethan kneels beside him watching him pack.

"It's about the adventure," Ethan says.

"Of course it is," Abel snaps back. "Unlike most of us, you came from somewhere better off." Abel pauses for a moment, fixing a glare at Ethan. "My mother is a widow. Once she became one, she inherited all of my father's det. My greedy landlord, as well as my father's boss, is having her work the debt off, which she can never repay. Lord knows what else he is making her do. Ser Kodak found me as he was grabbing a lead from his contact there and offered me the chance to get her out."

Ethan's voice becomes subdued. He mumbles, "I'm—"

"What, sorry?" Abel cuts him off. "Don't be. Isn't your fault. Just realize that nothing is getting in my way, and certainly not a two-day trip to some dark cavern."

Ethan nods, squatting with his hands interlocked together. "Well, I'm certain we'll find something down there."

Abel stands, slinging his gear over his shoulder. "Something definitely is down there."

"What makes you so sure?" Ethan pops up to join him.

Abel points to where Ser Kodak is gazing at the horizon from the cliff. "That's his second cigar for this morning, his body seems tense and he's pondering. He's anxious, not nervous. Ser knows something worthwhile is down there."

"So why send us?" Ethan asks.

"Because he knows it's dangerous, but he wants to see how dangerous it is." Abel shrugs. "Or maybe he just isn't feeling it."

"Well, he's sending his precious project with us," Ethan states.

"True. It wouldn't surprise me if Cleo provides surveillance too." Abel rubs his chin. "Either way, we'll have to be careful."

They stand there for a moment, gazing at the waving lights in the sky weaving among the clouds. Soon the clouds dissipate like feathered mist and the rays light up the sky. Although it is considered morning, the nearby sun is relatively dim compared to most solar systems, and the amazing moon is still there, bits of the surface causing meteorites to fall on Promethium, displaying a beautiful performance of streaking light across the sky.

"It's beautiful and terrifying at the same time, eh?" Ethan says.

"Truly is." Abel mutters.

"It's almost as if we're right under Armageddon."

"Huh? I suppose so."

Abel gasps as he awakens, his heart racing. He takes in his surroundings. He's back at *The Tip of the Spear*. Was that a revelation? Was that what Zao's contact was talking about?

He pushes up from his cot and ambles to his wall locker. Upon opening the latch, his heart almost leaves his body. Eva is hiding in his locker.

"God... damnit, Eva," he says. "What are you doing in there?"

She sits hugging her knees to her chest like a small child. "Sometimes they don't find me in dark places like this."

"Right." Abel shrugs off her excuse and pays attention to the old photo on the inside of the locker door. The old photo of him with the other Collectors. "Where's Zao?" Abel asks.

She glances up at him with big eyes. "The market."

"We need to find him." Abel studies the photo.

"Why?" Eva asks softly.

Abel then turns the photo toward Eva and points at the destroyed moon in the sky. "I know where we need to go."

Chapter 11

Abel and Eva stride through the snow, the cold snapping at their ankles. "Loberon isn't bent on letting up the snow anytime soon."

Eva struggles to keep up with Abel, hugging herself in her thick winter coat. I'm not used to this intense cold. Space station life is usually temperate. The cold is biting my skin with fierce intent."

Abel steps up his pace, his gaze bouncing around the outpost searching for Zao. The breakthrough has caused him a headache attached to a slight adrenaline rush. Whatever this may be—the skull, Aegis 12, this woman—It's all connected to his dreams. It's connected to whatever happened on Promethium.

As they tread through the snow, the lit-up structures of the outpost surround them. The workers and residents conduct business as usual, the brutal cold apparent on their rough faces. Life out here is brutal, and the cold weeds out the weak.

Soon they reach the marketplace. Rather than stalls, it's

a collection of small buildings with neon signs. Several shops offer food and produce, others offer gear and trinkets, and some sell all forms of entertainment and vices.

Faint laughter comes from the distance. Between two buildings, Zao wearing his oversized coat over his robes, talks with a taller stranger. Tucked in his arms is a familiar container—the pill-shaped canister containing the Starskin debris that he found next to his remains.

Abel's blood boils inside him. Eva sees him too, her anxiety evident in her tenacity to bite a cuticle.

How dare he? How dare he take my score beyond all this? Abel's mind clouds with rage as he marches toward the scene.

Zao's laughter halts as he sees Abel marching toward him. "Now I know what you're thinking—"

"What the hell is this?" Abel stands before them clenching his fist.

"A deal," Zao states with a calm posture. "We need fuel, food and units, unless you forgot."

"Oh, I didn't forget." Abel's jaw is clenching now, then he turns to the stranger. "Who the hell are you?"

The stranger is even taller than Abel, and he wears a rugged cloak with a hood that hides most of his face. From what Abel can see, his faces show signs of a well-travelled man. He sports a short red beard and a ruddy complexion. "Just an interested buyer," The stranger replies with a flat tone.

"Ah." Abel eyes him for a moment. "At least tell me you aren't low-balling my associate here who is trying to take my score."

The stranger lifts his arm to show the digits on the data pad on his arm. The sum causes Abel to pause and glance at

Zao. "This is for the expedition?"

Zao nods. "Yes, one hundred percent."

"Okay." Abel takes a step back from the stranger and Zao resumes the transaction.

In a moment, the transaction concludes and Zao hands over the canister to the stranger.

"Pleasure doing business," the stranger mumbles and walks away.

"Likewise." Zao turns and encounters an unexpected slug to the face. The force from Abel's fist sends Zao face-first in the snow. Blood leaks from his nose and paints the snow, despite his efforts to stop the bleeding.

Abel stands over him shaking his hand. He wipes blood from his knuckles. "Don't sell my scores under my nose again."

Zao spits a mouthful of blood onto the snow and looks up at Abel with a grim face, "Noted."

Abel nods. "Now, since you were out cheating me, I've been—"

"Sleeping?" Zao chimes in.

"No," Abel replies. "I mean yes but having a revelation." He pulls out the photo from his chest pocket and shows it to Zao, once he has found his glasses. Zao adjusts his spectacles and peers into the photo.

"Is that you?" He asks. "And is that old man wearing your coat?"

"Yes, and yes. But look at the sky behind us."

Zao gazes deeper into the photo. "What's with that moon? Wait… where is this?"

Abel sighs, then replies softly, "Promethium. My first gig."

Zao pushes himself off the ground. His nose is no longer

running with blood, but he still pinches his nose. "Wow, your first? What's the deal with it?"

"Remember what that woman said? She browses art underneath Armageddon."

Zao thinks for a moment, then shakes his head. "You think she's on Promethium? That's a stretch. The place is in another system and no one ever leaves there."

Abel shakes his head. "How many places do you know that has a destroyed moon rotating the planet? Listen, this is my skull, my remains. This woman knows something about it. That is why she told you. She knew that I would come to you, and she knew that I would eventually find this out. It's something in my dreams, my memories."

Zao scoffs. "Your dreams, huh?"

Abel sighs. "Yes. Every time I sleep I have a dream about my time on Promethium. The thing is, I never see the end of it. Usually I wake up to a woman's voice, telling me to wake up. Yet, this time, I didn't hear her."

Zao stares blankly at Abel, then mutters through his lower swollen lip, "So obviously something is up with your mind."

Abel rubs his hair and leans against the wall. "I don't know."

Zao turns and starts a slow shuffle through the alley. "Well, I'll be on the ship taking advantage of your med kit. Looks like we're heading to Promethium, but you two are doing the errands," he calls out before disappearing around the corner.

Abel exchanges glances with Eva. "Was punching him too much?"

Eva shrugs. "At least blood is warm."

Abel can only stare at her lips when another outrageous

reply flows out, but then he shakes out of it. "You're an odd one, but at least you're honest. C'mon, you're coming with me on these errands."

Eva gazes up at him with her fist clenched against her chest. "Can we get noodles? My friends enjoy noodles."

"Um, sure. If there are any." Abel trudges through the alley with Eva close behind.

They spend the day bartering with vendors and fuel men. Abel and Eva restock on rations, new E.V.A. suits, and water and oxygen tanks. The outpost has everything the traveler needs, it seems. In its own charming way, the outpost is a sanctuary against the brutal cold.

Yet, Abel knows all too well that this comfort is only temporary. That is the benefit of being a traveler, One can find niches of comfort in brutal places. Being here fuels his fear of settling down. He fears that once he does, he'll lose his enthusiasm and his spirit to the mundane of the moment. Much like the locals who surround him.

Eva, on the other hand, treats the world with extreme caution, yet with overwhelming curiosity. She examines trinkets and products in the stalls, listens too closely to the conversations between locals, and occasionally covers her ears and shuts her eyes, as if something is shouting at her. Then again, remembering what Natasha has said about Eva and her condition, perhaps something is screaming in her ear.

The two finish the majority of the errands and come across a noodle stand. They sit down to enjoy their meal, and the noodles with the spiced broth refresh their bodies and strengthen them against the bitter cold. The odd duo barely share any words with each other, but the broth seems to calm Eva's nerves. Abel decides to break the silence, once Eva seems calm. "So we have one more thing to do before we leave."

Eva looks up, her spoon halting in midair. "Hm?"

Abel leans in. "We need warp fuel. We have everything else we may need, but Promethium is in another system, and that requires warp fuel to reach. In Promethium's case, lots of it. The planet isn't exactly close by."

Eva nods, staring with wide eyes as she slurps in a noodle. Abel returns the gaze, searching for signs that she's listening.

Then Eva speaks up. "Why do you carry it?"

Abel tilts his head. "Carry what?"

"Your skull."

Abel glances around. If anyone were to hear these two foreigners talking about carrying remains, that could cause unwanted attention. Abel leans in and whispers to Eva, "I don't know. Just feels strange. Almost as if I need the constant reminder that this is real."

"What is considered real and fantasy?" She whispers back.

"Well, it should be more black and white. What is here and in front of you versus what you can touch and feel."

Eva shakes her head. "I have been struggling with reality my entire life. Reality is as tangible as any material. It can be shaped and sculpted, fabricated, and put on display."

"I see." Abel ponders the thought.

"Like your mind, for example," Eva adds.

"What do you mean? Like how yours is?"

"No." Eva pauses for a moment to slurp in another noodle, then glances up. "When you threatened the fake monk with my syringe, you stumbled back."

Abel recalls his slight panic attack in the laboratory.

Where he had his split-second flashback of being surrounded by lights. Being cold and alone, and feeling a needle pressed up against his own eye. "Yeah?"

"I've seen it once before. The memory is an interesting advantage we have in this universe. Yet like any other, it can be tampered with like yours."

Abel's eyes widen. "You think my memory has been tampered with?"

Eva nods.

"That's absurd," Abel says, but then his mind trails off. Could it be? Could his mind have been tampered with? Memories deleted? Or memories planted? One thing is for sure, someone is controlling his life. He is now more committed to find the woman on Promethium.

"Is it?" Eva asks, staring at Abel. "You've found your own body, your own end. Is it such a stretch to say that your mind has been modified as well?

"I suppose not."

Eva nod. "What did you see?"

Abel scrunches his face trying to remember the key details. It was so sudden. "Lights…and a needle."

"A needle, hm. What did you feel?"

"What did I feel? I felt cold… and lonely. The brightness of the lights almost gave me a headache…and then pain. Intense pain."

"I see." Eva ponders for a moment.

"What does that mean?" Abel asks.

"Ever since you've found that skull, your memory may be coming back to you in response to certain triggers. One can try to erase memories for a long time, but they are never truly gone."

"You're saying that what I remember isn't real, and my

true memories will come back in split-second flashbacks?"

"What I'm saying is—the key to solving this is in your mind," Eva responds with her usual soft voice, but this time it's tinged with an eerie ghost-like quality.

They sit there in silence, both almost finished with their noodles as they feel the cold harden their skin and thicken their blood. Finally, Eva wipes her mouth, then pops another question. "I think we're missing an important detail."

"And what is that?"

"Why Aegis 12?"

Abel thinks about the planet for a moment and recalls his near death from the radiation. Why Aegis 12? What is so special about the planet? The heavy radiation and toxic storms would keep any sane person away from it. The planet stinks of death and madness. Sure, there's the *Starglider* wreckage, but those can be found on other planets.

"I suppose I haven't asked that myself," Abel says. "The planet is a shithole, nothing but dust and radiation clouds. The planet literally almost made me rot before I reached my ship."

"I can see." Eva glances at Abel's blister scars.

Abel notices and rubs a palm on his cheek, feeling the tiny craters on his face. Will they ever heal? Regardless, Abel shakes the thought. "It doesn't matter how many questions we ask. The next step will be to get to Promethium and find that woman. There's not much else that we can do."

"Oh, don't worry—" A thick, Sovlikian accent pierces Abel's ear, and then a large hand slaps on his shoulder.

Startled, Abel turns to face a grizzled man with a mechanical eye. Towering over him, his eyes look crazed. "Vadim?" Abel murmurs as two other Satyr Militants approach Eva from behind and startle her as well. One, a woman with a scar across her cheek and a buzzcut, and the other a plain-looking man with stubble on his face. All of them look like they have seen hell, which is understandable.

"I believe you have something of ours," Vadim states as coldly as the air attacking their skin.

Abel is surprised that some of the Satyr Militants survived the attack on the compound— even more so that a group tracked and found them. Then again, it's not like they've gone far; they were forced to land somewhere on Loberon, so the Satyr Militia must've caught up fast.

"So everything went well at the compound?" Abel smirks and sips the last of his broth. The bowl goes flying when Vadim throws his fist across Abel's jaw.

"You were there." Vadim cracks his knuckles. "You saw the result of your betrayal, and stealing our D.N.A. scrambler."

Abel spits some blood on the ground and wipes his mouth. Looks like bad karma. He remembers delivering justice to Zao not too long ago. He squints up at Vadim. "I didn't steal your D.N.A. scrambler. She came willingly. Besides, the compound wasn't exactly a hotel resort anymore."

"How did the Federation know of our compound's location? Was it you?" Vadim demands as he sets his hands on the table.

"Ask Sergei." Abel spits on the ground again. He exchanges looks with Eva, who is now chewing on the nail of her baby finger as the woman still grips her shoulder.

Shit, of course they're armed. Then again, he is too. He still has the Hudson in his coat, but he would love to avoid a gunfight if he could. He can't predict the outcome, and Collectors live long by not taking unnecessary risks. These remnant Satyr Militants are hot-headed from losing plenty of their brothers and sisters at the compound. If they didn't want blood before, they sure do now.

Vadim leans his face close to Abel's, and his hot breath attack Abel's nostrils. "You bastard. He was my brother. You killed him and Natasha."

"What? No." Abel shakes his head. "They killed each other. Your brother ratted you guys out. I would have nothing to gain from risking my neck in the middle of your precious base."

"Bullshit." Vadim raises his hand until Eva speaks.

"It's true," She almost squeals, causing Vadim to pause and turn his attention toward her.

"They killed each other, Vadim." Eva speaks softly. "Sergei betrayed us."

Vadim is visibly distraught from the words and steps away from the table. Abel releases his breath, his cheek throbbing in pain. The other two militants step away from Eva, their faces grim. A day ago, they had a family and were fighting for a noble cause, at least in their eyes. Now family and cause are squashed like cockroaches by a government that will most likely forget their existence next week.

Abel sighs and leans forward, resting his hands on the table. "Look, I know how it feels. Everything your people worked for just got burned to ash. Yet we had nothing to do with it, and Eva came with us willingly."

Vadim peers at Abel and nods. "I should've known."

"Yeah well, shit happens." Abel scoots his chair back. "Where will you go now?"

Vadim shakes his head slowly. "I don't know. The Federation may try to squash stragglers. I'll have to move, along with these two here," he says and waves his hand toward the other two militants.

Abel nods, pressing his lips together. These people were expecting to deliver at least some vengeance today and preserve what they have left. They have lost nearly everything, and now they must go on the run.

"Where will you go?" Vadim asks, eyeing Abel and Eva.

"Well," Abel scratches his head. "I came to Eva to help me with some research. We're still on that."

Eva nods. "In pursuit of the truth," she says.

"Right, what she said." Abel says.

Vadim's demeanor seems to lift slightly, "The truth? To exploit the Federation's evil policies and acts on its people?"

"No." Abel exchanges glances with Eva. Vadim wouldn't understand the mystery that they're trying to solve. "Everyone knows how terrible the Federation is. Thing is, I think everyone's just accepted it."

Vadim lets out a soft chuckle and a defeated sigh. "Amazing how powerful the word 'terrorist' can be, huh?"

"Truly." Abel replies and pats him on the shoulder. "We should probably split ways. You do have the Federation on your tail."

"Yes, perhaps that will be best." Vadim lifts himself out of the chair. He then lifts a finger to his ear and speaks, "Wolf-1, let the fake monk go. We're moving out."

Seems Zao has had better days.

"Sorry about that," Vadim mutters, then turns his attention toward Eva. "Good luck, Doctor Morgan, I hope that these men benefit from your unique insight as much as we have."

Eva nods in response.

"Farewell." Vadim marches off with the other two militants.

Abel feels a fresh gale almost knocking him sideways, then turns toward Eva. "We should probably get going."

The duo travels back to the ship and find Zao sitting on one of the rusty camping chairs in the hub. The chair seems to be losing the battle against his weight.

"We had some visitors recently." Zao glares at the two.

"Yeah, they caught us at the noodle stand," Abel replies. "But we talked things out, so we shouldn't have to worry about them."

"I'm fine, thanks for asking." Zao's face shows major signs of frustration. "They pointed a gun at my head, Abel."

"You act like that's new to you." Abel shoots a sly smile.

Zao only glares. "What's next?"

"Next we need warp fuel. We can't leave the system for Promethium without it. Know any depots around here? I've checked and there's nothing."

Zao pinches his chin with two fingers, then his eyes widen. "Yes, there's one here on Loberon, but—"

"I'm not going to like it," Abel cuts him off.

"Yeah, there's a depot controlled by the Federation. It's going to be locked down tight after the compound raid."

"Shit," Abel whispers to himself and leans against the wall. "No black-market dealers around here?"

Zao shakes his head. "Not that I know of. This system is too far out."

"There is another way," Eva says. The men swivel toward Eva, whose arms hug her chest. "Does anyone recall the battle of Uvir?"

Abel shakes his head, but Zao replies, "I know Uvir, another dead planet at the edge of the Sovlikian system, although not as deserted as Aegis 12."

Eva nods. "The Satyr Militia had a listening post on the surface of Uvir. It was also a refueling station for outgoing ships. Which also included what we need."

"Warp fuel," Abel chimes in. "Why is 'included' past tense?"

Eva bites her lip. "The outpost was wiped out. A ground assault with a dogfight above Uvir's atmosphere. There were no Satyr survivors. The Federation abandoned it soon afterwards."

"So, what's the point of us going to a wasteland with a destroyed outpost?" Zao asks.

"Because the ships that were in the dogfight—they were fueled to leave the system."

Abel digests this news, the hum of the ship providing background noise. The outpost most likely has crashed ships around the landscape. If they were fueled to leave the system, their warp fuel could be salvageable. "This could work," he says. "Either we risk heading to the Federation's warp fuel station and get arrested, or worse. Or we head to Uvir to try to salvage it, but there is no guarantee that we'll find any."

Zao scrunches his face. "It would be safer if we go to Uvir. No need to risk going to any Federation post."

"Then it's settled," Abel's voice echoes through the ship. "We're plotting a course to Uvir. Everyone strap up."

Chapter 12

The night cannot become more beautiful than this.

The thoughts ring through the mind of the masked man, gazing up at the destroyed moon on a planet that now seems to be in a long dark night. Promethium displays darkness in a most beautiful fashion reflecting light off its destroyed moon, the lights dancing across the sky.

The Keeper stands in a courtyard, gazing into the sky with the moonlight reflecting off his black mask. The courtyard surrounding him is constructed of stone with alien flora decorating the area. Shades of pink, purple, and dark blues dot the courtyard, matching Promethium's landscape, although the colors are lost in the darkness. He insisted that the laborers construct the courtyard using simpler methods and materials. Nothing prefabricated. With his wealth, authenticity is essential.

"Keeper," The familiar, soft voice breaks the silence.

The Keeper pivots to focus his attention on Cyra, who seems to have a companion with her. A hooded man with a red beard carrying a pill-shaped canister under his arm.

"Ah," The Keeper's modulated voice rings to the stranger's ears, "Our listener has arrived. What of our precious experiment?"

The stranger nods. "Keeper, they are now leaving Loberon and currently in search of warp fuel to leave the system. My sources tell me they are plotting a course to Uvir."

"Uvir…hm." The Keeper's mind trails off, then returns momentarily. "I remember Uvir. Brutal place, but habitable. Yet only for the strong."

"I have also bought the canister from them, as you requested." The stranger offers the container.

The Keeper gently takes it from the stranger's hands and opens it, the lid emitting a soft hiss. The dim, reflective light of the Starskin shines across his mask, The Keeper's eyes wide from the canister's beauty.

The stranger leans forward and peers at the mask. "May I ask why you want this?"

The Keeper lifts his head in response and stares at the stranger in silence. Then he replies, "It is the proof of angels. Thank you, my listener. There's a ship waiting for you. You may go now."

***

The stranger's face scrunches, but he remembers his payment. Too high for him to be asking questions. Still, the mysterious aura The Keeper emits makes any person uneasy. He doesn't know how Cyra puts up with this eerie atmosphere. Perhaps she sees something in him, or they have a much longer past together.

The stranger makes his way out of the courtyard, and a tall servant walks past him on his way out. Constructed of metal and wire, the servant's eyes emit blue lights, the lack of humanity apparent even on its faceplate. Still, it moves with elegance and purpose.

***

The Keeper hands the canister to the servant, entrusting it with its care. "Please take this. There should be enough to begin."

The servant gently takes the canister and bows in response. Its joints whir with movement, and it circles to depart the courtyard.

The Keeper then turns to Cyra. "Please, walk with me."

The pair strolls along the courtyard without speaking. Her heels click against the stone, and the apocalyptic moon shines over them. The Keeper moves in silence, his hands interlocked behind his back.

"Keeper, why are we still hoping that this man, this Abel, is what we need?" Cyra finally says.

"You know very well, Cyra. He's the one who can activate what we need." The Keeper replies, looking straight ahead.

"You know what terrible things he has done. What makes you think that this Abel can change?"

"Yet, you know what I have done as well."

"That is different."

"How?" The Keeper stops and turns toward Cyra.

Cyra returns The Keeper's gaze. "Because you are aware of your actions. This one chose to forget."

"And look where I am. You see what that has done to me."

Cyra frowns, then she changes the subject. "The latest piece of Starskin from Abel, will that be enough?"

The Keeper nods. "Yes, it should be enough. Now we need one last ingredient."

Cyra becomes silent for a moment, her brows forming a furrow. "The catalyst."

"Yes, the catalyst." The Keeper answers under his breath. "The key ingredient to activate what we need. Do you remember where your grandfather hid it?"

Cyra's silent thoughts are legible on her face. "He hid it on Uvir."

The Keeper lets out a brief chuckle. "Well, I suppose that is a humorous coincidence. Perhaps you can also retrieve our dear Abel."

"You want me to bring him? I thought you wanted to wait for him to find us?"

"I did, but my condition worsens every day." The Keeper stares at the moon. "We need to travel soon. The longer I stay idle the more my body betrays me."

Cyra bows her head. "As you wish."

The Keeper swivels to face Cyra again. "We are so close, Cyra. Bring him here, and whether or not he'll comply willingly makes no difference."

"I will not fail." Cyra spins around and marches out of the courtyard, her heels echoing through the cold stone.

Chapter 13

The wind is still, and the air is quiet. The remains of once proud fighters litter the landscape. Crashed star fighters act as landmarks through the empty landscape. The wind carries ash across the ground, whistling lightly to fill the quiet space.

Uvir… a world of ash, scrap, and the whispers of the dead.

The quiet breaks with a loud crack in the sky. The clouds dissipate, and engines roar, interrupting the vast nothingness. Piercing through the heavens, *The Tip of the Spear* makes its entrance into the dead world. The engines crackle as the ship comes closer and closer to the surface, dipping and careening, the effects of Abel's careless driving. Though reckless, his reckless maneuvers are intentional and efficient in helping him save fuel.

Soon, the power of the engines is enough to cause a cloud of ash to form on the ground, and the ship slows while extending its landing gear. As the engines whir and the ash blows in all directions covering the wreckage below, *The Tip of the Spear* finally kisses the ground with its landing gear.

The ship lands, and the engines begin to simmer as the ship relaxes onto the surface. The ash settles and forms a ring around the landing sight. Finally, the boarding ramp of the ship opens, and the unlikely trio stand there with rugged gear and scarves around their faces.

"Well, this place is quaint," Zao says, his voice muffled through his scarf.

"We're just here for the fuel, nothing more." Abel descends the ramp with Cleo hovering by his side in her usual spectral hawk form.

"The dead is especially talkative here," Eva mumbles from behind.

True, Uvir is quiet. The trio scan the environment surrounding their landing zone. A field of crashed fighters dot the landscape. Off to the distance, they spot a much larger wreckage, a frigate of enormous proportions.

"We should certainly find warp fuel in that frigate, if we don't find it in the fighters," Zao says while pushing his ankles through the ash.

The air is not too hot, not too cold, and is actually pleasant on his skin. Although ash floats in the air, the masks help with breathing. Yet, each planet brings its own challenges, and Uvir's challenges are not obvious. Based on Abel's experience, those planets usually turn out to be the deadliest. "Cleo will help us search the wreckages," he says. "Let's get moving."

The trio wander through the graveyard. The air rests so silently that the quiet sits uneasy in their ears—something about exploring ruined places such as this. Abel thinks back to the conflicts that cause these environments. He's often explored old outposts, abandoned mines and facilities, and even ancient ruins. He trudges through trying to fight the silence with his unquiet mind. Just like on Aegis 12, even in this vast open space, he can almost hear whispers carried along the wind. Like in the dark cavern, the graveyard surface of Uvir speaks.

He glances at Eva, who seems to be more afflicted. Shivering, she hugs herself and scratches her triceps. "You okay?" Abel asks.

She turns toward Abel. "They are especially active here."

Abel nods, familiar with the feeling. He has seen it with other Collectors. They display it in different ways in different environments, but it is the same emotion. Fear.

"I know," He says, then looks ahead.

Cleo hovers over the wreckages and scans the scraps of metal, which display no signs of any warp fuel salvageable from the wreckages. They make their way among the carcasses of aluminum and steel, hugged by mounds of ash. The corpses of pilots and crewmembers are nowhere to be found.

Zao waddles in front for once, then turns to shout back, "We may have to go to the frigate."

Abel thinks for a moment. He's right. Fighter squadrons are connected to a fighting frigate, a much larger ship. If they had to warp to another system, the fighters would dock in the frigate and warp that way. "Let's do it. Everyone stay close. I'm not liking this place for some reason."

"You've been in some dangerous places, Abel. Why are you antsy about this place?" Zao roars back from a few meters in front of him.

"I don't know," Abel replies. "Something about it... I just don't know."

The trio, plus Cleo, eventually reach the frigate, a marvelous colossus of engineering and aerospace, all collapsed onto the surface of a dead world. The ship's main fuselage is split into two, with debris scattered throughout the landscape. The trail behind the frigate forms a valley of destruction. Cargo containers litter the crash site, and various pieces of furniture and equipment create obstacles around the wreckage.

The trio enter the crash site and are greeted with a jungle of scrap and deformity. The metal moans while rust eats away at the scrap, and the electronics inside the ship have long since been silenced. This was once a proud frigate, now its carcass a memorial of service.

Abel turns toward the group and addresses them, "Okay, any warp fuel is going to be in the engine bay. We're looking for canisters that hold antimatter. We should be able to carry them easily. Just be careful if you find one. If we break the housing container, we'll all be fried."

Zao and Eva nod their agreement. The frigate wreckage seems almost haunted, and everyone in the group proceeds with caution.

An hour passes, and the group roams through dark corridors and haunted rooms. Every corner displays evidence of life with unused equipment and beds with scrambled sheets. Ash coats the walls and furniture with a thin layer, so they keep scarves over their faces. Eva jumps at shadows and twitches through the dark halls.

Zao waddles through the corridors, not bothered by the space. The corridors are surprisingly wide and spacious, and he seems the least bothered by the wreckage. Then again, Zao is only a concierge for Collectors. He doesn't actually visit the gig sites; rather he points Collectors to them. His naïve nature shows.

Abel watches both Eva and Zao ramble through the site, and he feels a large sense of responsibility. Many years ago, he wore their boots, following an older man in ruins and remnant sites such as this. Although his group with Ser Kodak was large, he remembers how it felt following someone into uncertainty. The fact that these two have willingly agreed to assist him in finding the truth to his potential murder, he feels something new and strange—a sense of companionship.

Cleo scans the corridors, trying to detect items of interest along the way, as well as threats. For a while, Cleo hovers idly, lighting the way through the darkness and acting as a guide.

"Look at this." Abel walks toward some signs on the walls of the corridor. "The engine bay is close."

"Good," Zao replies. "Because I am getting exhausted."

"Welcome to the gig, my friend." Abel chuckles softly. "How does it feel to be on the ground?"

Zao rests his hands on his knees. "I guess…exciting? Yet I feel like my chest is becoming sore."

"That's called exercise," Abel remarks. "You'll get used to it, I think."

Suddenly, Cleo's hawk projection becomes bright red.

The group freezes at the sudden change, and Cleo emits soft beeps.

"What does that mean?" Zao whispers, his body frozen in place.

Abel scans the corridors, then turns toward the group. "We're not alone on this ship."

"Wait, what?" Zao whispers back, yet Abel disregards his response as he pulls out his Hudson H9.

Eva and Zao jump back at the sudden draw of his weapon. They don't understand that when a Collector encounters someone else at a site, rarely are they willing to split the spoils. Yet rarer still that he's had to use his sidearm.

The group inches down the corridor. Cleo stops when they reach a larger engine bay, a massive compilation of machinery and monitors. The monitors remain black and the engines are as cold as stone. The air is still, and ash coats the mechanics inside the bay. Every step seems to echo throughout the engine bay, causing the group to gasp with every step.

"Cleo, where are they?" Abel whispers to the hovering sphere.

Suddenly, a soft voice sounds. "Neat A.I."

The group whirls toward the voice, and a woman emerges from the darkness of the machinery. The woman carries a messenger bag, and a scarf envelops her head. She's pale, yet her skin is fair, despite the harsh environment that surrounds them.

"Who are you?" Abel demands, hiding the slugger behind his back, yet his posture remains straight and confident.

"Another Collector." The woman replies, matching Abel's posture. "I'm here for a gig. Question is—what gig you are here for?"

Abel doesn't break his attention. Eva and Zao remain still, watching for any sudden movements.

"Warp fuel," Zao speaks out from the side. "Warp fuel supply has been restricted in this system."

"Tell me about it," the woman says. "Yet I'm sure this frigate has some salvageable."

"What are you here for?" Abel asks without blinking.

"Something different," the woman answers. "Not warp fuel, but something unique on this ship."

Abel tilts his head. "Unique?"

"Yes. This frigate was actually transporting some unique cargo that could be profitable if returned."

The woman reaches into her messenger bag, and Abel tightens the grip on his slugger. To his surprise, she brings out a canister for everyone to see, a small one glowing with a purple haze. Warp fuel. "Help me and I help you?"

Abel relaxes. Turns out warp fuel is salvageable here and this mysterious woman has a canister. Perhaps the only canister. Still, they don't know what she is looking for and why she wants their help. Despite her willingness thus far, Abel still proceeds with caution.

"Okay I'll bite. What do you need?" Abel asks.

The woman gives a slight smile, "I'm looking for something on this ship and I may need help getting to it. Help me out, and you can have the canister and a share of whatever we find."

Abel shoots a glance at Eva and Zao, seeing if there's any concern on their faces. Zao shrugs in return, and Eva bites her pinky. He turns back to the woman, "Okay. But before we get started, what's your name?"

The woman replies, "Call me Cyra."

"Okay, Cyra," Abel remarks. "Where are we heading?"

"The bridge. There are some logs that I want to extract. It'll be much quicker with your help." Cyra heads toward the exit. "May I ask who all of you are?"

"I'm Abel, and this is Dr. Eva Morgan and Zao. And this here A.I. is Cleo."

Cyra nods. "Abel, hm. Not that common of a name

anymore."

Abel shrugs. "Guess my mother liked uniqueness."

Cyra chuckles. "Well, in that case, Abel, let's head up to the bridge."

"Wait, just you two?" Zao exclaims. "What do you suggest we do?"

Cyra circles around to address Zao. "Perhaps there is more warp fuel around here, or something else of value. Splitting up will help us cover more ground."

Zao forces a grin and faces Abel. "Abel, a word please." He pulls Abel to the side and whispers in one of the corners of the bay. "I have a bad feeling about this 'Cyra.'"

Abel nods. "Listen, I know she seems odd, and I am just as curious and cautious as you are. But she has what we need, and it may be the only canister."

Zao sighs. "True, yet she seems off, but I can't figure out why."

"The mysterious stature and willingness to share," Abel ventures.

"Right. Just be careful and give us a shout if things go downhill." Zao hands Abel a small device, an earpiece. "We'll keep Cleo here, but here's something I picked up on Loberon so we can keep in touch."

"Aw, you shouldn't have," Abel says. He pushes the device into his ear, then moves to Cyra's side. "Let's go."

The newly formed duo now makes their way through the dark corridors of the once proud frigate. Silence fills the void of the space between them. Abel is cautious. He's never worked with another Collector besides Ser Kodak. He has always worked alone, excepting Cleo, and has always been cautious of other Collectors because at the end of the day, they're just as greedy as he is.

Still, he examines Cyra and can't help the feeling that something is off about her. Now and then, he catches her piercing him with her gaze, her dark eyes staring into Abel's soul. He recognizes that expression very well.

Hate radiates from her eyes.

With her tense stature and her malicious glances, why is she helping him? Also, what could she possibly want out of those files in this frigate? All answers that is he seeking, though curiosity will one day be his downfall.

Finally, his thought-ridden silence is broken when Cyra speaks up, "So, Abel, how long have you been doing this?"

"Doing what?"

"Collecting."

"Well," Abel's face scrunches. "Long enough to make me look older than I am, I suppose."

"Ah, the rewards often outweigh youthful looks," Cyra remarks. "What got you into it?"

Abel is silent for a moment, then mumbles, "Some asshole."

"Some asshole?" Cyra scoffs. "I guess many of the galaxy's problems start off that way."

"I guess so."

"So, who was this asshole?"

Abel doesn't know why, but he wants to share with her about his beginnings with Ser Kodak. Despite wearing the coat, the smell of synthesized tobacco seems oddly strong right now. "His name was Ser Kodak. Gentleman adventurer, seasoned Collector, and a guardian of history," Abel remarks.

Cyra smirks. "That's quite the title."

"That was what he told me when he picked me up from my colony. In reality, he was ruthless and flooded with ego.

Ser Kodak sacrificed novice Collectors for the sake of mediocre scores."

Cyra's expression changes, and her posture is less guarded. "Ah, then not so grand."

"No."

"What happened to him?"

Abel thinks for a moment. He hasn't exerted effort to remembering the fate of Ser Kodak in a long time. Still, as he digs through his mind for the details of his early career, the fate of his grizzled mentor is foggy. As if he can't remember. "He perished in a tragic accident, I suppose," he simply says.

Cyra nods without comment.

Why can't I remember? One would think he'd remember what happened to Ser Kodak, his grizzled old mentor. Then he recalls a conversation with Eva on Loberon—the conversation about his mind being tampered with. Does this have anything to do with Kodak? With what happened on Promethium? It is all an unlikely stretch. Then again, so is finding your own remains on an unexplored planet.

"You okay?" Cyra asks, obviously seeing the frown on his face.

Abel shoots a glance at Cyra. "Yes, of course. We should keep moving."

They reach the entrance of the bridge, the center of operations for the entire frigate. The electronics remain cold and idle, and the seats in the bridge are empty. Covered in a thin layer of dust and ash, the windows' glass appear opaque. The light beams highlight the dust particles in the air as Abel and Cyra cut through them. Cyra wipes a monitor with her gloved hand and examines it for any signs of function. She then pulls out a screwdriver from her bag and pries open a panel under the monitor.

While she tinkers with the wires and electronics, Abel decides to break the silence. "So, what exactly are you looking for, if you're willing to share more?"

Cyra continues manipulating the wires. "I'm looking for a lead actually. A file or a manifest. Something on this ship is valuable. I'm trying to find proof of it and its location on the ship."

"Ah, gotcha." Abel mumbles and stands to the side. Cyra works until the monitor shines with life.

"There we are," she says under her breath. Her fingers dance across the screen, analyzing the information.

"You know, I can get Cleo up here to work on that monitor to extract whatever info you need," Abel suggests.

Cyra stops momentarily and glances up at Abel with a forced smile. "No thanks, I got it."

"If you insist." Abel turns around and places a finger on his earpiece to check on his companions. "Zao, this is Abel, come in."

A moment passes, and he hears the familiar voice of Zao in his ear. "Hey Abel, everything good?"

"Yeah, everything is fine. We're in the bridge now. Cyra is extracting the files. Says she's looking for a manifest."

"Got it," Zao replies through the intercom. "Hey, listen, you know anything strange about this vessel?"

Abel pauses and looks around the bridge, then replies. "What do you mean?"

"I mean at first I thought this was a Federation frigate. Yet I may be wrong. And Eva says the Satyr Militia barely had a fleet, let alone any frigates."

"What are you saying, Zao?" Abel now says in a whisper.

"Cleo has been scanning the structure, and there are no signs that this is a Federation ship at all. I think this is a private vessel."

"That's not entirely strange. The Federation sometimes employs mercenary ships for their fleets."

"But this is a cargo ship. Yes, there are fighters, but there are no guns on this ship, and it's a little small for a combat frigate. Why was this ship here in the middle of a battle between the Satyr Militia and the Federation?"

"Wrong place, wrong time?" Abel suggests.

"Maybe," Zao continues. "Yet, based on my contacts from Station 17, no trade routes pass through here, so there's no reason for a cargo frigate to be anywhere near here. Unless—"

"Unless?" Abel adds.

"Unless they were smuggling something into or out of the Sovlikian system. Just keep your guard up," Zao says.

"Will do." Abel closes out and turns back to Cyra, her fingers tapping on the monitor.

"Almost finished," she says without breaking eye contact with the screen.

Abel nods, then wanders through the bridge of the frigate. His curiosity heightened, he searches for clues without appearing to do so. Everything Zao told him peaks his interest. If this was a cargo ship, why wasn't it following a trade route, rather than in the center of a massive planet conflict? What is its cargo and why is Cyra here after it?

These questions race through Abel's mind. His eyes dance around the bridge as he heads to the glass windows. His eyes wander over the landscape of Uvir. Such a barren wasteland, littered with scrap and ash. The front of the frigate looks like a destroyed city down below. Amazing how much design, engineering, and pure manpower must go into building these ships, only to fall out of the sky to the ground below.

The wind blows ash across the land, then he sees something off in the distance. Within the graveyard of crashed ships, someone sits elegantly among the corpses of scrap. Another ship, sleek and magnificent and the shade of crimson. The ship resembles a blade sitting sideways, with a sphere in the middle that acts as the main fuselage. It must be Cyra's ship. And if so, she must be one successful Collector to have such an elegant and expensive vessel. Then something even stranger.

A second ship.

The second ship is not as exotic, perhaps a hauling ship. More rugged and not as aerodynamic, the ship is meant for cargo, either goods or passengers.

Abel's heart sinks. A second ship means a second pilot, so Cyra's not here alone. As he examines the ship from afar, Cyra's voice makes him start.

"I got it. I know where we need to go," she exclaims. "Turns out it is on this ship, and I even know what deck it is on."

Abel turns to face her with his arms crossed. "Who else is with you?"

Cyra shrugs. "Just me."

"Then why is there a second ship out by yours?"

Cyra and Abel stare at each other. That is, until Cyra pulls out a pistol and points it at Abel. "Listen to me closely, Abel. You are going to comply, willingly, which will make this easier for both of us."

"Dammit," Abel mumbles and raises his arms, but he doesn't break eye contact with the woman.

"I'm here for an important artifact. Two, in fact. I was hoping to acquire one before moving on to the other, without you making a fuss."

Abel's body remains frozen in place, his eyes analyzing Cyra's stance, searching for an opportunity to turn the situation around in his favor. In order to do that, he has to keep her talking.

"Who are you really?" Abel asks, his hands still raised.

Cyra's eyes water. "Well, I thought you would recognize me, Abel. My name is Cyra. My full name is Cyra Kodak," she says.

A muzzle flashes from her energy pistol.

Chapter 14

Digging through random containers on a crashed frigate isn't what Zao had planned for his week. Rummaging through scrap and expired supplies is taking a toll on his lungs, as well as his muscles.

Eva sits on top of a closed container, yet her body remains twitchy. Why Abel brought her this far along, and why she has agreed to stay, is beyond him. Zao breathes hard and leans against one of the containers. His body slides down the side of the container and his legs fall beneath him, leaving a trail of sweat on the container.

He sits there for a moment, panting. Eva shoots him a glance. "Tired?" She asks.

Zao's breathing isn't getting any easier, and his face is so hot it feels like it'll explode. "You could help out."

Eva lifts a shoulder. "Chances are Cyra has the only warp fuel canister, and she's using us to get what she needs. There's no point in looking for another canister."

Zao lets out an exhausted, yet disappointed sigh. "You

may be right. I may not know Cyra, but I know her type. Do you think something's off about her?"

"Something seems off about all of you," Eva replies. "You Collectors are bizarre."

"What can I say? It's a risky business." Zao pushes himself off the ground and waddles about the containers. "High risk yet high reward often create paranoid and mysterious characters."

"How did you and Abel meet then?" Eva asks.

Zao lets out a brief chuckle. "Oh, what a day that was. He was young. Well, at least younger than he is now, of course. Collectors start out young. They're often brought up by mentors and come from places of struggle or unrest. Abel hails from a colony where people owe a lot of money to powerful people. He never told me what colony that was, nor did he tell much about his mentor."

Eva nods. "He doesn't share much?"

"About his past? No. He was always a neutral man. Always accepted the universe for what it is. Abel never bothered about politics or relationships or connections. Always, and I mean always, he's had one goal."

"And what would that be?"

"He worries about the next gig. The next score. Most Collectors his age, those that make it as far as he has, often talk retirement. Him? No. Not a peep about retirement. He always asks for the next one."

"Sounds like he's running from something."

"Maybe." Zao bows his head, lines framing his mouth like brackets. "In this business, you don't ask too many questions about someone. As long as they keep bringing in units."

Eva stares at nothing, seeming to digest the information

Zao tells her.

Zao shrugs. "Abel is one of the best. He could've retired a long, long time ago. He's smart and curious, but he refuses to settle. For me, that works out just fine."

Eva nods. "What exactly do you do for him?" She asks while scratching her arm.

"Well, I'm what they call a concierge. I make contacts, gather intel for leads, and give them to other Collectors for a small share of what they find." Zao sighs, then continues, "My family is a long line of smugglers. Ever since the first light-speed voyagers launched off out of China."

"China?" Eva tilts her head.

"Oh yes. An ancient province from Earth. From a long time ago."

Eva nods, her eyes wandering, taking in the darkness of the engine bay.

"What about you?" Zao asks.

Her eyes dart back to him. "What?"

"Why are you with us? You had the option to abandon anytime. You had the choice to go with Vadim and the rest of the Satyrs. Why us?"

Eva's head is still, yet her eyes dart around. "I've never been alone. They whisper to me. Yet when you two came along and reminded me of Abel's mortality, I saw a chance."

"A chance for what?" Zao asks.

"A chance for connection. For friends. Outside of my—"

"I think I get it." Zao nods.

"Yes. The Satyr Militia found me and saw my skill set. They brought me along and provided me a small family, or so I thought. But they only wanted me for one thing. I've helped cover their tracks."

"How do you know Abel and I aren't doing the same?"

Eva shrugs. "Like I said… a chance."

They study each other for a few moments, then break eye contact to peer around the darkness. The engine bay occasionally lets out metallic moans, echoing like the spectral cries of a dead ship.

Until a loud metallic clank rings throughout the bay.

Eva springs off the container, her head twitching around, searching for the source of the noise.

Zao shrugs. "Something probably fell—"

"No," Eva shushes him. "Something is here."

Then they hear it. Quiet at first, then progressively louder. Metallic footsteps approaching them, and Cleo pops up from a bundle of containers, a red hound this time.

"That's a little heavy for a human," Zao whispers. He places a hand on Eva's shoulder and pushes her behind a container.

They peek over the top of the container, and Cleo eliminates her holographic projection to hover beside them. From the darkness, a large figure emerges. Constructed of steel and wires, it moves with elegance and purpose, Its eyes glowing in the dark with an orange haze.

"I don't think that's from the frigate," Zao whispers. "I knew something was off about Cyra."

The figure scans bundles of stacked crates and containers, obviously hunting for something. Or perhaps hunting for Zao and Eva.

The trio remain silent, waiting for the figure to pass. Zao presses his finger to his earpiece, trying to reach Abel. Yet there's only silence from Abel's end. "I can't reach him," he whispers to Eva.

The figure then shifts the containers that Eva and Zao are hiding behind. It strides to their cover, examining each.

Behind it, three armed figures emerge. Although their gear is mismatched, they carry the same weapons, and their helmets emit the same three lights in a triangular pattern. With goggles glowing red in the darkness, the figures communicate with one another in low, modulated voices. Still, it doesn't prevent their voices from sending chills spiraling through Zao.

Who are these guys? He huddles beside Eva. The large robotic figure moves closer to the containers. The armed figures meander through the area, their hushed voices echoing through the bay. The robotic figure breaks away from the containers when one of the armed soldiers waves it over.

Zao and Eva study them from their hiding spot. The armed figures' uniforms are high-grade. Normal clothing peek from beneath their high-tech protective armor. Scarves protrude from their vests and cover their necks. Full black helmets with goggles protect their heads. The large robotic figure moves among the three of them, as if it leads the squad.

"Shit," Zao whispers. "They're contractors."

"What do we do?" Eva whispers back.

Zao shakes his head. "Keep hiding and try to get a hold of Abel. There's no way we can survive a fight against these guys."

Suddenly, a plasma repeater sounds behind them. Zao spins to find one of the contractors charging toward them, his rifle's three barrels rotating slowly.

"Oh shit, there's a fourth one," Zao mumbles to Eva, who hovers close.

The contractor touches the side of his helmet, and a modulated voice reaches Zao's ears. Then the other three contractors approach their hiding place, and the robotic figure towers over them, staring down at them with red eyes.

"I am Servant," the robot states. "Please do not resist."

Chapter 15

A gentle, familiar breeze returns to caress Abel's skin. The air is crisp and clean, rejuvenating his nostrils. He inhales deeply. Once again, he's back on Promethium.

This time he stands before the entrance of a large cavern. The darkness inside is pitch black, swallowing any light that dares shine past its entrance. The leaves gently float along the wind, carried by the whispers in the cave.

Ethan joins Abel's side as the other Collectors converse in a group off to the side. "What do you think is in there?"

Abel only shrugs. "Who knows, but whatever it is he wants it bad."

Ethan nods and turns to the other Collectors. "Hey, Let's move in."

The other Collectors chat among themselves and join Abel and Ethan. As a group, they approach the entrance of the large cavern, the darkness swallowing them along with the light. The stress of the dark quickly takes hold of the group. A couple of Collector novices start to shake, their breathing heavy.

In a moment, Cleo lights up the dark by taking the form of a holographic hawk. Her blue, spectral wings wave in magnificence as it guides the expedition. The other Collectors gasp at the sight, and even Abel is impressed by Cleo's display thus far.

"Ain't that handy?" Ethan remarks. He stares at Cleo for a few moments, then clears his throat. "Let's keep moving."

The radiance Cleo displays illuminates the moist rock faces of the cavern. Drips of water echo through the empty dark, and the wind still carries, piercing the ears of the group with light humming. The setting is unnerving. Abel and Ethan lead the group, with the others covering the rear. Cleo hovers in front, lighting the way further into the cavern.

The further they travel, the more the walls change shape. From jagged rock faces they morph into chiseled walls and columns. Then the walls display symbols etched into the surface. Unrecognizable etchings smother the walls along with odd, geometric patterns.

"What is this?" Ethan mutters. He runs his fingers lightly across the surface.

"I don't know, but I don't recognize any of the markings," Abel replies.

"Hey, Cleo." Ethan turns to the spectral hawk. "Could you scan these markings?"

Cleo emits an affirming beep in response and hovers closer to the wall. The scan displays several rays of light moving up and down, highlighting the etchings. After several moments, Cleo gives a negative beep in result.

"No result?" Ethan asks.

"We may be some of the first humans down here," Abel suggests. "We should be careful when we go down further."

"Maybe this is what Ser Kodak is after? The writing on

the walls?"

"Perhaps, but I feel like there's something further down. The writings definitely mean something, but I doubt it's the only thing this place has to offer."

"What do you think this place is?"

"I don't know. A ruin of a city? Or a place of worship?"

Ethan rubs his jaw and thinks for a moment. "Well, I'm not seeing any structures that show signs of anyone living here. The place-of-worship theory seems more feasible."

"I guess we'll know more further down," Abel adds.

"In that case, after you." Ethan extends his arm, ushering Abel to the front.

Abel obliges and takes the lead, trailing Cleo and facing the dark firsthand. The space in the cavern widens and breathing becomes easier. After a few minutes of trekking, Abel nearly trips over his own feet. Then he sees it. The carved steps.

The group notices as well, and echoing footsteps fill the air as they climb up the stairs. The steps seem to multiply, and their breath becomes labored.

"How many of these damn steps are there?" Ethan calls out from the back of the group.

His question is answered when Abel reaches flat ground. The last step brings him to a platform high in the cavern. From what he can tell, he seems to be standing on a pyramid-like structure. The other Collectors soon join him at the top along with Ethan. They lean forward and find Cleo hovering next to an object resting in the middle of the stone platform.

"What is that?" Abel whispers underneath his breath.

The group approaches the object slowly, toward Cleo who hovers around the object, scanning it with great intent.

The object radiates with a shimmer of light, twisted in a beautifully sculpted form. It stands about as high as their hips, and the top is pointed like a dagger.

"It's an obelisk of some kind," Ethan states. "Cleo seems interested in it. Could this be what Ser Kodak is looking for?"

"I think so." Abel replies. "Yet he only sent us down here to verify its location. I wonder why?"

"It was going to be dangerous? But coming down here was a breeze."

Abel gazes at the obelisk and finds himself drawn to it. The longer he stares, the more the radiant light shimmers in waves through the obelisk's surface. Then he feels his mind being picked, and hushed sounds—voices are whispering in a language he doesn't recognize, something ancient yet elegant. They're calling to him, yet he can't understand them. Calling for him to reach out. The whispers drown out the voices of the group around him

He reaches a hand toward the obelisk.

"Abel," Ethan says to him, "What are you doing?"

Abel ignores him while entranced by the obelisk. His gloved hand nears the spearpoint tip of the object, the whispers becoming louder in his mind. The other members do not share the same trance, and their concern grows as Abel's hand nears the obelisk.

"Abel, I don't think you should touch that." Ethan calls out, but his words have no effect. Abel touches the tip of the obelisk, and the entire group flinches.

Nothing happens, and Abel's trance fades. "What happened?" Abel says, his voice groggy.

"I don't know," Ethan replies. At the same time, the wall's etchings illuminate the entire cavern. The symbols light up with a blue haze, the obelisk illuminates golden rays, and the entire chamber is lit with a holy haze of luminescence.

The Collectors explore the chamber, the symbols reflecting off their eyes like stars in the night. The walls also display mysterious dotted patterns and lines.

"What is this?" Ethan mumbles. His wide-eyed gaze scans the chamber.

"A map, I think," Abel suggests. With his last word, a massive pressure and pain descend on his head as if it was splitting in two, and a migraine pours in like a rushing river. He grabs his temples, grinds his teeth, and moans. Slowly, he collapses onto the floor, the voices of the Collectors distant.

"Abel," Ethan exclaims, running to his side with the others. Abel groans, shutting his eyes to block out the intense light.

Suddenly, the images flood him—odd constellations and acts of God. Stars dying and reborn, fabrics of realities being torn and worlds being destroyed. Images dart by like cosmic rays. Realities collapse and stars dim, then shine bright. It's as if he's witnessing the creation and experimentation of universes, and his mind wants to melt.

Then he sees it. Holes torn apart in dark space and fleets of chariots passing through the gateway. At first, they seem like smooth comets shining with the same radiant light as the obelisk, then they extend out massive sails like ships on a dark and empty sea. The sails expand like angelic wings in the heavens, absorbing the energy from the stars.

Abel's body seizes. His nose bleeds, and his body shakes violently. Ethan and the expedition scramble to call for help through their comms, and then one by one, their noses bleed.

One Collector screams and grabs her head in pain. One by one they fall, their bodies convulsing on the floor.

Ethan shouts into the comms. "Ser Kodak, we found it. But the whole expedition is seizing. We need immed—" His body betrays him. Foam oozes out of his mouth and blood spurts from his eyes. A seizure caused him to drop onto the floor.

All of the Collectors, including Abel and Ethan, writhe or convulse on the floor. Then after an eternity, their bodies become still. Their eyes stare at nothing and their bodies begin to cool, their blood pooling around the obelisk. Ethan's body lies motionless, his eyes wide open, their exuberance vanished.

Except for Abel, whose body still shakes. His eyes dance like loose marbles and his mind races like two comets. Until finally, his body becomes still. Unlike the others, his eyelids close, and his body remains warm.

***

Ages pass, and Abel wakes with a sudden gasp. He examines his surroundings, expecting to be back home. Instead, he's in the cavern underneath the surface of Promethium. The cold bodies of his colleagues surround him, and the one closest is Ethan. A pang of grief strikes him—his only friend is dead.

He lifts his head. The chamber is still lit with symbols and patterns. Yet now, he understands. The patterns, the dots, the symbols—all together, they make up a plan. A plan for something greater, something deemed only achievable by God.

He scans the chamber. Not all are dead. Cleo hovers next to the shoulder of the man who brought him here. He stands with watery eyes, his arms limp at his side. The man kneels down and places a hand on Abel's shoulder.

"Now you see, don't you?" Ser Kodak speaks with a soft voice this time, which is just as unsettling as his usual grunt.

Abel nods and replies, "What did I see?"

Ser Kodak only smiles. "Why, you saw the beginning. You saw our angels." He stands while Abel soaks in the words. He peers up at his mentor, who's pulling a pistol from his coat.

The sudden draw of his weapon brings a collective gasp from the others. Ser's cold eyes gaze around the chamber, seeing the youthful faces that he convinced to join him on this expedition, and manipulated their enthusiasm and their ambition to his advantage. But he now has what he needs.

He glances down at Abel. "Angels that only you and I can know."

He then raises his pistol to the nearest Collector, and the flash from it lights the chamber. Sudden cries from the young Collector ring out and all the other Collectors scatter for cover. It is hopeless. Ser Kodak is quicker, and he guns them all down like dogs in the street.

The flashes light the chamber, and the booms of the pistol pierce Abel's ears. Once it is done, Abel's ears ring and the bloody bodies of his colleagues surround him. They only wanted a better future. Now, all are dead and soon to be forgotten beneath the surface of paradise.

Abel's body shudders, his voice is mute, and his mind is fogged. His dream has never progressed this far before. *Is this all real? Why am I dreaming of this now?*

Ser Kodak stands, a grim shadow over his face. The smell of iron and synthesized tobacco fills the air as he walks back toward Abel, stepping with care over the bodies. He again kneels beside Abel, his words filled with grim gentleness.

"My boy, we're going to open the heavens. One day, you will see the value of my mission."

Ser's eyes pierce into his soul. His reality is slipping, his consciousness warping back into reality.

Chapter 16

Abel's consciousness begins to return to him. The cold, steel floor reaches through his trousers. They must be dragging him by his coat. As soon as he can see his surroundings, he recalls the flash from Cyra's pistol. He feels around his body, checking for bleeding. Then he lets out a grateful sigh, until he realizes something else. He can't move his legs.

"Relax," Cyra says. "It was a paralysis blast. Although I wish it put a hole in your skull."

"Yeah well, tell that to the Abel that was on Aegis 12." Abel remarks, sarcasm dripping from every word.

Cyra scoffs, "Oh, there is so much you don't know."

"About that, what the fuck is going on?" Abel exclaims. "I follow a lead to a toxic planet, I find a *Starglider* wreckage with my corpse lying next to it, and now you're dragging me through the corridors of a frigate. You, Cyra Kodak."

"That's right," her tone frigid.

"Didn't know Ser Kodak had a daughter."

"Granddaughter, mind you," she snarks.

"Regardless, what do you want from me?"

"From you? I want you dead. But my employer wants something else from you."

"And who would that be?"

"Someone too powerful to name. No one you need to know as of yet." She tugs on his trousers to continue their trek through the hall.

"In that case, what are you looking for here?" Abel asks.

"You for one. Also, the catalyst. Or the method to activate it."

"The catalyst?" Abel frowns.

"All in good time."

They finally reach a large room scattered with cots and beds. Supplies from the opened cabinets litter the floor. A sign on the wall blinks, still legible although some of its letter aren't illuminated, showing that this is the infirmary.

"Here we are." Cyra drags Abel through the clutter.

Abel examines his surroundings. How is she pulling him like a bag of feathers? Also, why is Ser Kodak's granddaughter holding this massive grudge against him? Who is this employer that she mentioned, and why does he want him? Abel tries to recall his memories past Promethium involving Ser Kodak, yet he can't. Why can't he remember? His mind feels as if it's collapsing into itself. He grabs his head, forcing himself to think. Cyra turns and glances at him.

Finally, they stop at an odd bed. A metallic cot with numerous straps, rings, and a small device toward the end where the head would be.

Cyra slides the bed from the machine. To Abel's

surprise, she actually lifts him onto the bed with one arm. She must lift. Unable to move his legs or chest, she easily straps him down.

"Funny thing about my grandfather," she says. "He was involved in more than just collecting treasure and artifacts. He used that fortune for more controversial exploits. Memory manipulation, reality fabrication, and the study of the fabric of time and realities."

Abel can only stare as she continues talking. A fresh wave of dread, humiliation, and helplessness fills him. All he can do now is listen to Cyra.

"You, good Abel, have taken advantage of at least a few of those projects."

"What do you mean?" He asks.

"Don't worry, you'll find out." She grits her teeth and tightens the last strap, then her eyes narrow. "Do you know where we are?"

Abel shakes his head. "I only know that this is a frigate that was in the wrong place at the wrong time."

Cyra shakes her head. "Maybe, but this ship was the research vessel of Ser Kodak."

Abel soaks in the revelation, his heart suffocating, drowning. "W-what?"

"Yes, I know. What are the odds?" Cyra chuckles. "Well, I suppose the odds aren't that slim, since it was I who gave Zao the lead to Aegis 12."

"It was you?" Abel gasps. "Why? Why all of this for me?"

"That is the same question I sometimes ask myself." Cyra says with a soft sigh. "There is so much for you to learn. Nay, for you to remember."

Cyra taps the screen on the side of the machine, and to

Abel's surprise, it lights up. After a few more taps, the bed of the machine moves further inside, surrounding Abel with metallic rings. Lights shine bright inside the rings.

Metallic arms grasp his head and force it to stay still. Soon after, a much smaller metallic arm extends out and forces the eyelids of his right eye to open. His eye begins to feel dry and then to water. Slight panic overtakes his body.

"I know that you can still move your head and arms, but I'm going to need you to restrain yourself," Cyra says, dancing her fingers across the screen.

"What the hell is going on?" Abel demands, his voice echoing off the walls.

"Like I said, you're going to remember. Also, the catalyst I mentioned, it isn't an object. It's something inside that my grandfather saw fit to bestow upon you a long time ago. Congratulations, Abel, you are the catalyst. This machine is only a means of making it a reality."

Before Abel could open his mouth to spit out more questions, the whirring of a mechanical device catches his attention. The device reveals a large needle slowly descending toward his eye. He flinches as it descends closer, closer. Panic takes a hold of his body. Whatever muscles he has control of squirm out of the straps. Yet, his efforts are worthless.

"Don't move your eye. It's critical I get this right." Cyra glares onto the screen.

Abel has never felt so helpless, so cold, and even with Cyra standing to the side, he feels alone.

Then he remembers...

I have been here before.

What did they do to him? Why is his mind blank when he thinks past Promethium? The questions race through his mind like cosmic rays, as the needle comes closer and closer to his eye. He grits his teeth, hoping that somehow, he can get out of this, as he always has in the past.

This time it doesn't seem to be that way, as the needle penetrates his pupil. To his surprise, he doesn't feel immense pain. His face, his lips, and his body freeze. His mouth gapes open. The needle injects a compound into his eye.

In a moment, he sees images. At first, familiar images of his old companions, of Ser Kodak, all flash as quickly as light. He then sees images of blood, of violence. His old companions standing before him, then flashes of death and betrayal. Finally, immense chaos, of stars dying, of worlds collapsing, and reality bending.

The images change. They become personal. Images of him in different scenarios. Yet they all occur in unfamiliar places, but they all end the same way—with his death.

The flashes stop. The needle slowly retracts. A small stream of blood oozes from the wound, then stops. The metallic restraints also retract, allowing him to move his head. He blinks several times, feeling a massive headache take hold of him. The bed slides out of the machine, and he finds himself face-to-face with Cyra.

"So—" she begins. Cold eyes warmed by hate. "How does it feel… knowing what you did?"

Abel is stunned by the dozens of revelations that just passed through his mind. All so fast, accounts of the things he's done. Dozens of emotions hit him at once. Mourning, sadness, utter shock. The emotions combine into nothing. Blank as the dark, empty space. Cyra's speaking. He slowly turns to face her, gritting his teeth against the migraine.

"I would gladly do it again—" He clenches his fist, yet a tear falls down his cheek, betraying him.

Cyra eyes him but says nothing. Abel can't tell if she expected his answer or if he fueled her hatred. Perhaps both.

"Fine. That doesn't change the fact that we still need you. But you know what you did, so I doubt you'll come willingly."

She undoes his straps, and a group of armed soldiers with a tall, mechanical droid march into the infirmary. Abel manages to look up at the group—four armed guards and the droid, along with his two companions.

"Try anything, and they die," Cyra states as she unbuckles the last restraint. Abel lifts himself off the bed. Zao and Eva stand there, watching him, probably wondering what ordeal he just went through. Zao's face shows obvious confusion, and Eva's eyes dart around the room. Abel examines the group more closely, trying to count the armed soldiers and the tall droid. Then he spots something missing.

Where is Cleo? He quickly scans his surroundings. Cleo is nowhere in sight.

"What's going on?" Zao blurts out, only to receive a whack to his jaw by a contractor's rifle.

"Enough." Cyra raises her hand toward the contractor. "We're not savages."

Zao holds his jaw and massages it. Cyra kneels down to him, then glances up at his companions.

"Your companion here, Abel, is a monster. However, we need him for what we're planning because my grandfather thought it was a marvelous idea to put the catalyst in his mind."

Zao grimaces. "The cata-what? Wait—" His thin eyes now widening. "You're the one who gave me the lead for Aegis 12."

Cyra gives a slight smile. "That's right. We needed Abel

to come out of his hole, and you were the only one who could reach him. Not to mention, we needed more Starskin to finish our project. Which was an added bonus."

"What project?" Abel demands. "And why send me to a toxic planet if you needed me?"

Cyra then turns back to address Abel. "The Keeper, my employer, wanted to see if you were still capable of handling the task. He's articulate in that sense. Besides, it's not like you haven't been there before."

Abel clenches his fist, now remembering everything. The reason why they need him, and the reason why the finding of his own skull was actually the second time he was on Aegis 12. He remembers everything now. So much, too much, for him to unravel in front of his new companions.

Yet, there is one more detail that is still a mystery to him. "Who's this Keeper you mentioned?" He asks.

Cyra smiles. "You'll meet him soon enough. He is anxious to see you again."

"Again?" Abel asks.

Cyra opens her mouth to respond when the sound of one of the contractors shouting in pain interrupts. The droid known as Servant has one of its metallic hands around a contractor's throat, lifting him to the air with his feet kicking desperately. Then, a loud snap of the contractor's neck and his body dangles lifeless. Servant throws the contractor to the ground.

The other three contractors and Cyra back up, while Zao and Eva dart for the nearest cover.

"Please do not resist." Servant states as it walks toward another contractor.

"It's been hacked," A contractor yells, points his rifle toward the droid and opens fire. The plasma projectiles leave burn marks on the metal alloy, yet the droid marches on.

Abel spots Cyra aiming a pistol at Zao and Eva as they run for cover. He slams his body against her and throws a fist down upon her, but she deflects the blow. Abel is surprised by the strength of Cyra, then immense agony shoots through his hand as she crunches the bones.

"The Keeper said to bring you back, but he didn't specify about your health." She throws Abel off her body and springs to her feet. Abel slides across the infirmary floor. He tries to find his footing.

The contractors continue to fire at Servant, with its bright red eyes glowing. It marches toward the nearest contractor, grabs his rifle and swings it across his helmet. The contractor lays on the ground, dazed. Servant sets its foot on his neck, applies pressure, then tosses the plasma rifle to Zao.

***

Zao catches the rifle and begins firing at the other two contractors. The three rotating barrels blast with the bright fury of a god and sends the other two contractors retreating for cover. He may not be a good shot, or tactically trained at all, but he can at least keep them pinned down for a few moments. Sweats drips down Zao's face, and his heart begins to race. His adrenaline tunnels his vision toward the flashes from the muzzles of the barrels. The weapon shakes with fury and becomes hot in his hands.

***

Eva crawls from cover to cover, scooting closer to one of the dead contractors. She spots a holstered pistol and reaches for it. One of the live contractors spots her from his cover. He aims his weapon and fires. Blood splashes on her face from the contractor's corpse, and she leaps backward. Eva runs her hands through her face and body, checking for wounds. The contractor continues to fire at her position until Zao focuses his fire on the contractor's cover.

***

Abel faces Cyra as she approaches. She marches ahead with a confident gait, but her smile is sinister. Cyra is much stronger than he, her strength almost inhuman. She cuts a strike at his face, but he ducks.

He holds his crushed hand and backs away from her. Ducking and dodging, searching for a weapon to use. He feels for his Hudson, which she must've removed from him when he was unconscious. His eyes dart around the infirmary, looking for a weapon. Then, he spots a scalpel on the ground and grasps it in his left hand. As Cyra approaches he swings the scalpel at her, but she raises her arm to block.

That is when he sees it, her flesh open from the cut. But rather than blood, a dim light radiates through the wound. That color pattern, he has seen it before. The same light that shines like the debris he found on Aegis 12. "How in the—" He stares at her wound until she grabs him by his coat and lifts him off the ground.

"It disgusts me that you wear this," she growls, then slams him against the wall with a thud.

The air escapes his lungs from the impact. He struggles to his feet, coughing and gasping. Cyra approaches again. His thoughts race. Does she have Starskin arms?

Abel now knows that he can't fight her directly. Her strength and apparent hand-to-hand training outmatch him. But he has an advantage. Cyra is so fueled by pure hatred she's oblivious to what is happening around her. Abel scans his surroundings. Contractors have Zao pinned down, and the other Contractor is focused on Servant. Eva is crawling toward one of the corpses again to grab a weapon. Then Abel realizes that's his chance.

Abel sprints away from Cyra toward the firefight. He needs to lose her in the crossfire and join his group. She may have Starskin arms, but that doesn't mean she's blasterproof. Or is she?

Cyra apparently notices him moving toward the fight because she picks up her pace and darts in his direction. Eva manages to grab the pistol from the dead contractor's holster, then tosses it toward Abel as he dives for the weapon. Reaching out, Abel's hand makes contact, and he spins around to point the muzzle at Cyra.

Her cold features change to shock, as flashes erupt from the pistol. She ducks for cover while Abel fires until the weapon overheats. Abel keeps firing, scooting back toward the same cover that Zao hides behind.

Drenched in sweat, Zao also fires until his weapon overheats. Abel scooches beside him as Zao retracts behind cover. Then the other contractor returns fire. They both jump away from the plasma fire, and their cover heats their backs.

"You have a lot of explaining to do," Zao yells in Abel's ear in the midst of the plasma fire. His face is tomato-red, his breath coming in spurts.

"First we get out of here." Abel yells back, catching his breath. He rests his broken hand in his lap as his pistol cools down, almost ready for use.

Then quiet. The blaster fire stops. A moment of peace and clarity fills the air. That is until Cyra's exhausted voice interrupts the peace.

"Enough," She yells. Abel and Zao peek from their cover. Cyra has one arm around Eva's neck, and the other arm points a plasma pistol at her head. Servant's body lays on the ground, sparks flying from its head. The other two contractors stand beside Cyra and Eva, weapons pointing in Abel's and Zao's direction.

"Now—" Cyra starts, catching her breath. "That was fun, Abel. Come over here. Her life for yours."

Abel freezes. He looks at Eva, her eyes wide with fear, yet she remains silent. Cyra's cold eyes remain fixed on Abel, waiting for him to decide. Abel pauses, then raises a pistol toward Cyra and Eva. "Here's how it will go. You kill her, and I start shooting. You may kill both of them—"

"Abel?" Zao cries out. "Are you insane?"

"But you can't kill me, can you, Cyra?" Abel's voice is calm and cold, yet his heart races.

Cyra snarls and her finger presses the trigger. He continues, "Because you kill her, and I will most certainly make sure you have to kill me."

Cyra only stares, then, "fine," she mutters. Without breaking her gaze, she commands one of the Contractors, "Give it to him."

Like a drone, the Contractor pulls out a canister with a purple haze from his pack. He rolls it toward Abel. Warp fuel.

"You have a week. Or else she dies." Cyra and the contractors step back, making their leave with Eva.

"You know where to find us."

Next thing they know, Cyra is gone, along with Eva.

Abel stands in silence with Zao in the dark infirmary. The adrenaline running through his veins simmers, and his heart slows. As he calms, exhaustion and pain set in. Abel locks eyes with Zao, almost at a loss for words for what just happened.

Finally, Zao mutters, "What the hell is this?"

Abel sighs. Then he massages his forehead and replies, "It's about time I told you about my mentor."

Chapter 17

Back on *The Tip of the Spear*, Zao tosses the plasma rifle on the center hub's table, and Abel kicks out a camping chair and collapses onto it. He lets out a deep, exhausted sigh and sinks into the old chair. Cleo takes the form of a cat and rests on the center table.

"Okay, so—" Zao starts with his hand raised. "Let's hear it."

Abel is silent for a moment, gathering his thoughts and memories together, which now flood his mind. "My mentor's name was Ser Kodak. He was a seasoned Collector, one of the best. He picked me up from a colony that was poisoned by industry, where the people couldn't get out because we owed the corporations for everything. Well, Ser Kodak was pursuing a lead and was gathering a team. Much larger than usual for an expedition."

Zao leans against the wall with his arms crossed, fixated on Abel as he continues.

"This expedition was my first, and I left my mother behind, with the hope of bringing back a fortune and getting her out of there. But Ser Kodak was after something special in that expedition, and he was obsessed. His reason for gathering a large group of young and new Collectors was to use them for cannon fodder. The way to his goal was dangerous, and a lot of my colleagues were killed in the expedition."

Zao's face changes, morphing to uneasiness and pain as Abel continues.

"I found what he was looking for. An obelisk. Made out of pure Starskin. It was only as tall as my knees, but I was the one who found it and touched it. It caused my mind to fold. I saw things that were divine yet hellish."

"What was it?" Zao asks.

"It was a map."

"A map for what?"

Abel pauses for a moment, pondering how to word his response for Zao. He can't reveal too much to Zao. He's seen firsthand the kind of man this revelation brings out. If anyone else were to know this information, who knows what they'd try to do? Regardless, he needs to answer. "It's a map to navigate the universe in a more—how can I say—untraditional sense."

Zao blinks at his response, obviously not pleased with Abel tiptoeing around the full truth. Even though Zao is not entirely innocent of this himself, the events of the past few hours have transformed him into a man who tolerates less bullshit.

Zao uncrosses his arms, sets his hands on the counter, and leans his face closer. "Abel, you need to be straight with me. Eva was just taken by a crazy woman and some mercenaries."

Abel stands and paces a circuitous path around the room,

his hand pinching the bridge of his nose. The migraine from the machine is making his head feel as if it's being squeezed between two large hands. "The map allows someone to navigate the universe in a way that bends reality. It is destructive, and we can't let it happen."

"Destructive how?" Zao asks.

Abel leans against the wall, chewing his lip. "Do you remember the anomaly of the Helen System?"

Lines form on Zao's fleshy forehead. "Well yeah, it was one of the most tragic cosmic events in human history. The Helen star collapsed and swallowed its entire solar system."

Abel nods. "That destructive."

"That destructive?" Zao visibly swallows.

Abel's face is still as stone.

"How is that—" Zao begins to ask, then he sees Abel's expression. As if he remembers the event clear as day. "Wait, you were there?"

"Yup, Ser Kodak wanted to manipulate the universe. The Helen System was his experiment, and he used the map in my mind to do it."

Zao's eyes are as wide as plates.

"Now you understand why they can't get to me," Abel continues. "If they do, they'll manipulate the universe however they see fit, and they'll wipe the existence of worlds to do it."

"Why couldn't you remember any of this at first?" Zao asks.

"Because I wiped my memory to protect this secret. That machine that Cyra threw me in—I've used it before. It was one of Ser Kodak's side projects, memory manipulation. I took advantage of it and went into hiding. Well, the memory of me taking various Collecting gigs. Always moving and never stopping, so if anyone were to try to find me again, they would have a difficult time, to say the least."

Zao nods, then he glances up. "What about your skull? With the bullet hole?"

Abel pulls the container out of his bag and places it on the counter. The lid pops, and the hollow eyes look up at them. They stare at the grim skull for a few moments. "I did this," he whispers.

Zao's face snaps up to look at Abel, who stares at his own skull with a grim shadow over his face. "You killed yourself?"

"No, It was murder."

"Mur—what?" Zao shakes his head. "How in the hell?"

Abel mutters his response, "I guess it's like what Eva said, the universe is flexible."

Zao shakes his head. "Fine, don't tell me. But what about Eva? Are we going to leave her to hang? Or are we going to do something about this? Since apparently them getting their hands on you will cause the universe to collapse," he says, his words laced with sarcasm.

Abel crosses his arms and thinks about Eva. She has stuck with them the whole way ever since they picked her up from Station 17. She jumped on the opportunity to help them without even asking who they were.

"Surely she deserves more, Abel," Zao continues. "Cyra and this Keeper will kill her if we don't do something."

"I know." Abel cuts him off with a raised hand. "But we can't just barge in there. If they get a hold of the map inside my head, they'll use it for Lord knows what. Also, there's no guarantee that they won't kill you too."

Zao shrugs and gives a slight smirk. "I don't know. I sort of handled myself well back there."

"You got lucky is what happened," Abel corrects him. "If it wasn't for Cleo, you probably would have been shot." Abel circles the center hub, his chin resting on his hand. "We need a plan, and we may need help."

"Help from where? Who possibly can help us get Eva back? Also, who knows how many contractors Cyra has?" Zao taps his finger on the side of his face. "Any chance that Cyra would even honor the deal if you gave yourself up?"

"No idea. I knew Kodak, but not his granddaughter. He failed to have mentioned any of his family at all, so I have no idea about her honesty."

"Oh, do you think she's even a tad honest, Abel?"

He shrugs. "We can't know anything for certain."

"We need help. Armed help if we can find it."

Abel thinks back over his old contacts, but he draws a blank since erasing his memory and living in isolated drifting. Which doesn't leave him any room to meet anyone who's willing to raise arms for him in the future. Then he remembers Loberon, his encounter with Vadim. Vadim and a few survivors of the Satyr militia are now scattered across the Sovlikian System. If they could somehow reach Vadim— "What about the Satyrs?" Abel says. "If we contact Vadim and tell him that Eva was captured, do you think they would send some Satyr fighters to help us?"

Zao grimaces. The very thought of bringing radicals back into their business is the opposite of what he wants at this moment. "Are you insane? Those Satyrs have brought us nothing but trouble, and we can't risk giving the wrong idea to the Federation."

"They brought us Eva."

"That doesn't mean we should reach out to them for help. The risk is too great."

"So is abandoning Eva, and Cyra and The Keeper getting a hold of the map inside my mind."

Silence fills the air between them. The tense atmosphere of the situation makes the air in the center hub feel dense. Zao lets out a deep sigh, and Abel continues with his argument. "We need bodies with guns, and it'll be good since they'll want to rescue Eva. They respect her, and their army is mostly gone. What else are they going to do besides this?"

"Bold of you to assume that they're not off to some uncharted planet somewhere, rebuilding their little insurgency."

Abel shrugs. "Maybe, but it will be even bolder, perhaps idiotic if we go in with just us two."

Zao groans. "You're right."

"Thank you."

"But we don't have much time to make a decision. If we spend too long trying to find Vadim, they'll kill Eva."

"I know," Abel says as he looks down at his crushed hand—the bruising and one of his fingers dislocated. After the radiation on Aegis 12, the needle in his eye, and the crushed hand, he can't seem to catch a break.

Zao sighs heavily again. "She did a number on you. You should probably check yourself into your little robot infirmary."

"And what about you?"

"Flying us back to Loberon. Maybe Vadim didn't fly too far."

Chapter 18

Eva sits in the passenger seat. The elegance and swiftness of Cyra's exotic ship make flying easy. She feels as if she's one with the wind, whistling through the atmosphere like an arrow.

She hates it.

The Tip of the Spear's bumpy movements and ragged appeal helped keep her distracted. They distracted her from those voices that plague her mind—those voices that also uplift her spirit. A constant tug of war between two consciousnesses. Sometimes, it feels as if there are several.

They're not coming for you.
Don't worry, I'm sure they remember you.
They will slaughter you where you stand.
Remember, you can't give up.

Constant whispers bother her mind like rhythmic finger taps. Always as if someone stands behind her, whispering over her shoulder. It doesn't help that her hands are bound. The restraints digging into her skin cause her wrists to irritate and swell. As if she could do anything rash.

Cyra guides the ship through the air with ease. Her eyes fixate on the horizon that shines through the valleys between which she flies. The landscape is something to see, Eva thinks. Vibrant colors of the vegetation fill the scene like an ancient oil painting. Brilliant hues of violet and teal, shades of sea green and sunset orange make up the vegetation of this lustrous planet. This planet known as Promethium.

Eva peers out of the window. She tries to estimate the height of the trees, the thickness of the brush. The rivers and streams are almost crystal as they reflect an enriching blue. The mountains and cliffs carve into the landscape, making vast valleys, rich with waterfalls pouring over the mossy cliffs. All breathtaking in beauty.

The true treasure, however, is the moon in the sky. Visible even during the day, the moon is a marvelous display of destruction and magnificence. Large chunks have blown out, yet they still orbit the astronomical body. The destruction of the moon causes a shower of meteors to fall onto Promethium every couple of minutes.

Underneath Armageddon, they whisper to her.

Eva gazes up at the moon, its waving light reflecting off her pale face until finally, Cyra breaks the silence.

"We're approaching the estate now. Be sure not to make a fuss." Her fingers manipulate a screen.

Eva leans forward and sees a beautiful stone building with marble columns supporting the roof of the structure. Stone steps rise to the entrance of the estate from the front landing pad, and pots of local vegetation dot the property.

Cyra's ship hovers over the stone landing pad in front of the estate, wind blowing from the engines as she lowers it closer to the ground. Funny, the intensity of the wind blowing from the engines doesn't match the quietness inside the cockpit. Gracefully, the ship touches down with barely a jolt.

Cyra detaches her safety belt, stands and unclicks Eva's belt, and gently grasps her by the arm. The ship is not large, but the middle fuselage, which is a glossy black sphere, extends its ramp down to rest on the cold stone. Cyra escorts Eva down the ramp, while a contractor ship flies overhead, finding another landing zone away from their line of sight.

They approach the stairs leading to the entrance of the estate. The sound of her footsteps echo through the surprising, quiet air of the planet. Another fact that makes Eva uneasy is the gentleness that Cyra is displaying while escorting her. It's as if when Cyra's around Abel, she's ruthless and full of hate. But here on this planet and back to the estate, Cyra is at ease, with no evidence of her former posturing.

This isn't just her employer's home. This is hers as well.
Is this what feeling at home is like?
We don't have a home.
Don't trust them, Eva.

The whispers become louder in the quiet air, and her face winces and she squeezes her eyes shut. Despite her efforts, she can't shake them away. Perhaps that is why Station 17 suited her. Then again, she was never presented an opportunity to leave except when Abel and Zao showed up at her lab.

Eva and Cyra pass between the marble columns. The light of the destroyed moon reflect on the white marble. The soft wind of the planet gently blows dust across the stone. As the soft wind caresses Eva's face, they approach two giant wooden doors that make up the entrance of the estate. Eva raises her hands to touch the wooden surface. She has never seen wood before. Cyra swats them down.

"Don't, It's oak," She snaps.

"From Earth?" Eva asks under her breath.

Cyra doesn't bother to respond. The heavy doors open with soft silence to display the massive interior. Mysterious, luxurious décor fills the building. Ancient paintings line the walls and furniture, specially crafted from wood, fill each room. The same wood as the doors, Eva notes as they pass. Cyra escorts her through the unusual space.

Eva shakes her head. Days ago, she was in a littered lab with her sketches in an industrially-fueled space station. Now Cyra wanders through this mysterious, luxurious estate on a paradise planet, though her hands are bound.

Finally, they approach a smaller set of doors carved in a beautiful, runic pattern that she cannot recognize. Cyra pushes against the doors, revealing a wider space.

One wall of the room, made purely out of glass, allows light from the destroyed moon to peer into the space. Along the walls hang mysterious art pieces. Marble sculptures of nude human figures stand in the corners of the room. Eva stands in the center of this gallery, awed at every turn.

"Cyra, are the restraints necessary?" A ghostly, modulated voice erupts from out of sight. It echoes through the entire gallery, bringing goosebumps to Eva's arms.

"She put up somewhat of a fight. Just an added precaution," Cyra replies to the empty space.

"Nonsense. You should've known she would."

Eva focuses her attention on the voice, and then she sees him. A man with hooded black robes and a glossy black mask. He walks across the gallery floor with elegance, as if he is gliding across the surface. The only hint of humanity is the hazel eyes that peer through the mask.

The eyes. Why can't she stop staring at them?

The man glares at Cyra, now as still as a stone. "The restraints please."

Cyra's lips press together, and she moves to undo Eva's restraints. With a click, Eva feels the heavy restraints ease from her wrists.

"Thank you, Cyra. You may go now." The man waves his hand.

"As you wish, Keeper," Cyra murmurs and marches off, leaving the gallery.

Keeper? Eva turns toward the mysterious, robed man. This must be The Keeper that Cyra mentioned.

Suddenly, the whispers return.

Don't trust him, Eva.

He doesn't seem too bad.

A man of culture, perhaps?

His eyes—what do they mean?

"They speak to you often, do they?" The Keeper asks, cutting off the voices in Eva's mind.

Eva's eyes dart up, fixated by his question. *How does he know?*

"It's quite all right. I too sometimes suffer from an unquiet mind. Then again, it's not always suffering, is it?"

Eva says nothing. She shakes her head in response.

The Keeper returns her gaze. "Come, walk with me." He turns and strolls away. Reluctantly, Eva follows.

"I understand how the past few hours may have been difficult for you. Usually an elegant woman, Cyra often becomes intense when given the chance to encounter Abel. Perhaps even hurt him. I imagine that she may have roughed him up?"

Eva nods, keeping the pace alongside this spectral man.

"I often advise her not to. We only need what's in his mind."

"What is that exactly?" Eva asks, finally managing words.

"A map. A map to help navigate and manipulate the universe in a way that only the gods have the privilege of utilizing."

"What does that make Abel?"

"Still a man, one selfish enough to hoard the privilege for himself."

Before Eva can ask more, The Keeper leads her to a large painting. A horrific display of war and famine, four wooden panels painted in oil display a hellish scene. The middle panel shows a field of death. The corpses of men with ancient military gear litter the landscape, and a ragged skeleton hangs over the entire scene.

"Do you know this work?" The Keeper asks Eva, witnessing her unease. In response, she manages a shake of her head.

The Keeper nods, his hands interlocked behind his back. "It is *Der Krieg*, a work by Otto Dix. Otto was a German painter who fought in an ancient war centuries before the exodus of Earth. He painted what he saw, in order to show others the horrors that result from man's greed. He saw hell on Earth. Yet, men of power silenced his cries."

Eva can only stare. The work of art communicates a most haunted atmosphere. Yet as she gawks at it, her whispers remain mute.

"Do you understand what we're trying to accomplish here?" The Keeper asks her with a haunted voice.

Eva shakes her head.

A long pause passes as they study the painting, soaking

in the turmoil of the scene. Finally, The Keeper speaks. "I have dedicated my existence to making sure the greed of man doesn't lead to this ever again. The Federation squashes anyone who refuses their agenda. Colonies wage war outside of the Federation's influence, and men are willing to bend the universe to their will for the sake of wealth. I intend to end it all. I want to squash these men and their ideas, and I will end their reign."

Eva breaks her gaze from the painting and peers at The Keeper, finding that he is examining her closely for her reaction to his monologue.

"I want to create the perfect universe."

The perfect universe? The whispers return in Eva's mind.

Surely he can't be serious.

Perhaps he is the Messiah?

Nonsense, he is obviously a mad man.

Is a perfect universe even achievable? Should we take him seriously?

"I know it's a lot to take in." The Keeper continues and strolls to the massive windows where the light of the destroyed moon pierces through.

"A perfect universe?" Eva remains close to the painting. "Do you think that you can bend the universe to your will so that everyone can experience peace? You think that these worlds, these governments and societies, these systems won't oppose you? No one can control the forces of this universe. You're not the first to want this. Men who have pursued this goal often perished."

"Your time with the Satyr Militia has influenced your thinking," The Keeper replies while staring into the sky.

"How do you know me?" Eva demands. "I've only met

you today."

The Keeper becomes silent, his hands interlocked behind him as he watches Armageddon in the hazy sky. "Only today?" He asks.

Silence befalls Eva.

The Keeper then turns around to face her and approaches. "I know this feeling you have right at this moment. This feeling that you can't identify. It's the reason you couldn't stop staring into my eyes when you saw me. It is the same feeling that enticed Abel to take that wretched skull to the nearest space station. Call it curiosity. Call it whatever you want. Yet, sometimes curiosity merely covers the true intentions of our actions."

The Keeper pauses and stops in front of Eva. Eva's body begins to tremble, her knees feel weak, and her heart races with anticipation. Anticipation that attacks her chest as The Keeper slowly raises his hand and places his palm on his mask. He removes the mask from his face and pulls down his hood.

The revelation causes the whispers in Eva's head to transform into cries and pleas.

No, it can't be.
How is this possible?
Get out of here, Eva.
Run!

Yet, she's frozen to the spot.

The Keeper stands there in his unmasked glory. "That feeling is familiarity."

Eva opens her mouth, yet her voice trembles and words refuse to come out at first. Her heart despairs, and her body is numb. Finally, she manages, "How is this possible?"

The Keeper smirks, pausing before giving his answer. "I

suppose it's like you said once, the universe is flexible."

He passes Eva as she stares blankly at the floor. *How is this possible?*

The Keeper's voice erupts from a distance behind her. "Come, I want to show you something." His voice is no longer modulated. Now it seems more haunting than ever. Eva doesn't know how, but her foot takes a step and follows The Keeper.

He leads her to another large set of doors and pushes them apart to reveal an even larger area.

The space is twice the size of the gallery. Crates and supplies fills it. At the far end is another set of doors. A hangar of some sort. That's when she sees it. From the center of the room, shimmering rays of light reflect around the entire hangar. The object in the middle shines with angelic glory, its solar sails spread out like wings, and the main body is elegant and aerodynamically divine. It is the most beautiful thing she has ever laid eyes upon.

"I will tell you everything about my plans and the past that has led us up to this moment," The Keeper says.

Eva can't pull her eyes from the divine object in the middle of the hangar.

"Then after I tell you everything, we will become angels."

Chapter 19

The metal arms rotate around Abel's right hand like planets around a star. The purple flesh from the broken bones fade as the tiny nozzles spray a cooling mist on his hand. He feels burning, then tingling, then relief. He can't stop thinking about Cyra and her surprising strength—how she was able to stop his blow and break his hand with ease?

The Tip of the Spear rumbles as pulse engines boost the ship. The shaking calms him. He thinks back on the many years he's spent on the ship. His memory returning has brought up terrible memories, yet his time on this vessel isn't one of them. Abel has always loved this ship, ever since he laid eyes on it. Originally it wasn't his. The ship was one of the many vessels that Ser Kodak contained in his fleet.

Abel's hand twitches back to life. His fingers move, and the function of his hand revive. The color returns, although there still remains a shade of purple on his skin. He can clearly see the hand being healed. Although back to normal, the pain will be unforgettable.

After an hour, the metal arms and nozzles retract into the

medical kiosk by the bay area, one of many he'd had installed in almost every room of the ship. Travelling alone doesn't always allow for emergencies.

As he gingerly clenches his hand and opens it, feeling the immense tingling, strange music comes from the center hub. He stands and heads to the center hub.

Upon entering, he sees the portly man meditating on the center counter. Cleo hovers close to him, now in the form of a massive spectral butterfly, emitting a soothing tone to accompany Zao's hums.

The soothing aspect of the music is debatable. Abel lifts his arms in disbelief, then lowers them. "Really? On the counter?"

"It comforts me to be in an elevated position," Zao says between his hums.

"Yeah, well I eat there." Abel heads into the cockpit. "How far are we from Lobcron?"

"Not far. I suspect we'll arrive there in a few minutes."

"And you just left the cockpit alone?"

Zao opens one eye, the music continuing with Cleo's spectral wings flapping. "It's on autopilot."

"I see. So what exactly is your plan for finding Vadim and the other Satyr members?"

Zao sighs. "We scan the frequencies. See if they're communicating with each other. Then we trace them until we find them."

"If we find them," Abel retorts. "Zao, that can take weeks. We don't have time. It's not like we can just go back to that outpost and ask around. They may be long gone, and our source for their safehouses is captured. We may not have weeks to find the Satyr Militia—"

"Okay, okay I hear ya." Zao raises his hand. "Look, I've

thought about this, and we have a way to speed up the process."

Abel rolls his eyes. "Oh you do? And how do you suppose we're going to speed up the process? 'Cause our friend's life is on the line. "

"Oh," Zao says.

"What?"

"You said, 'friend.'"

Meditation music echoes through the ship. They sit in silence, then Abel shakes his head to snap out of it. "It doesn't matter. How are you going to scan the frequencies to find Vadim?"

"I'm not going to," Zao replies. He pushes to his feet, then points at Cleo. "Cleo is going to."

Abel glances at his assistant. He considers the possibility. "That can work, actually."

Zao nods. "Look, Cleo is an A.I., as you know, and I figure Vadim and his people have to communicate somehow. They could relay intel in code in the general frequencies. Since we don't land in Loberon but fly around in orbit to scan, Cleo will get a wider signal and pinpoint sources better without being in valleys and between mountains."

Abel nods. "Like a satellite."

"Exactly like a satellite." Zao points at Abel, like a lecturer to a student. "I don't know where you got Cleo, but she is a one of a kind. You honestly don't use your AI to her full potential. Now, it will take us weeks to listen to the frequencies for any patterns or code, but I bet you a few units that Cleo can analyze in real time."

"That's a bet I wouldn't take." Abel turns and heads to the cockpit. Zao follows him and sits in the copilot seat next to Abel. Cleo hovers, and the trio watch the stars zooming by like cosmic rays.

Zao's eyebrow form a V. Abel cuts him a sideways glance. "What is it?"

Zao opens his mouth, pauses, then speaks, "You said that the skull you've been carrying around--your skull—is evidence that you killed yourself?"

Memories flash of that fateful day. "I'd rather not revisit that."

"I deserve to know after coming all this way."

"You're the one who sent me to that planet."

"That you chose to trek anyway. Also, how the hell would I have known?"

Abel sighs. Zao's right. They both were to blame. Hindsight. It's time to tell Zao. "Fine. I mentioned the anomaly of the Helen System, you'll remember. It resulted in a tear in time and space. A gateway, in fact."

"A gateway? What exactly do you mean?"

Abel turns to Zao. Can he handle the burden of the truth? "What I mean is interdimensional travel."

Zao is silent, then snorts. "Are you serious? You mean, other dimensions and universes?"

"It's been a theory for centuries. Ser Kodak was the one who proved it. And he sent me to retrieve the means to accomplish it."

"And you are—"

"I became the means to accomplish this feat. As his experiments progressed, he finally solved the equation. The man was obsessed; it swallowed him whole, causing him to become irrational. The whole thing drove him mad."

For the first time, Zao is speechless.

"He finally was able to open a gateway, but he needed energy. Enough energy to cause a tear in the fabric between dimensions, and he couldn't do it on a small scale."

"What did he need?"

Abel lowers his head. *Why he is telling Zao all of this?* He swore to himself that he would never share this information with anyone. Yet here is, betraying his own oath. "He needed a star—one large enough to collapse into itself and create a mass with gravity so great it swallows everything, including light. Then it can spit the energy out into the neighboring dimension."

"You mean a black hole?"

"Precisely."

"Like the one that formed in the Helen System after the anomaly event."

Abel stares blankly into the monitor as a single tear rolls down his cheek. "Yes."

***

Zao is shocked by Abel's emotions. He has never seen this much dread before, as if the Helen System was special to him. That is when it hits Zao, like a punch in the gut. "The Helen System… that was your home?"

Abel nods. "Yes, it was."

Zao is beginning to understand why Abel is so reluctant to share his sudden remembrance. He lost everything from those events, including his home planet and his family. All because a man was obsessed with achieving a feat where men only theorized.

Abel's voice holds a tremble. "When Kodak opened that gate, others poured through. Other men who had the map in their mind. They were all…me."

Zao blinks after hearing this revelation. "You mean to say that other versions of yourself travelled from other dimensions?"

"Yes."

"So, how is that even possible? I'm sorry. This is all—"

"Impossible to believe?"

"Yeah, you could say that."

"I thought so too. Then I saw a group of other Abels, all conversing with Ser Kodak. All discussing a goal that was irrationally impossible."

"And what goal was that?"

***

Abel sighs. Even he still finds it hard to believe when he hears himself talk about it. "They wanted to achieve the perfect, peaceful universe."

Zao's eyes blink. "A perfect universe?"

"Yes. Ser Kodak's main objective. In order to do so, he treated it like any other science experiment—with trial and error."

"That would mean—"

"That would mean wreaking havoc in other universes, destroying solar systems and ruining lives—all for the sake of the experiment."

"So how did that lead you to this skull that was found on Aegis 12?"

Abel recalls the very moment he watched other versions of himself talking to Ser Kodak, all plotting to create a perfect universe by destroying others. That was the moment he decided he couldn't allow it to happen. "When the opportunity was right, I waited for them to congregate in one setting. At that moment, I killed them. I killed as many as I could—those that had the map in their minds and those that wanted to continue with the experiment."

Zao shook his head. "Where was this?"

Abel pauses for a moment to recall. "We were there. The frigate we salvaged at Uvir. Ser Kodak called it the *Congregation of Uvir*. I sabotaged the ship and brought it down to the surface of Uvir and took *The Tip of the Spear* to escape."

Zao's shock and disbelief are apparent on his face, but there's something else in his eyes—a newfound awe for his partner.

Abel continues. "There were, however, some stragglers after that. Some had survived the sabotage of the frigate. I had to hunt them down before they figured out the means of travelling back to their universe."

"Why couldn't they travel back through the black hole that was created in the Helen System?"

"They could, but even with the map, they needed a safe vessel to carry them through the rift."

"A vessel?" Zao frowns.

Abel sighs. "Do you know why *Starglider*s are so special?"

"Well, other than them being rare, the metal alloy they're made of is incredibly strong and resilient. Even though no one can forge them into anything."

Abel nods. "Ser Kodak found a way to forge Starskin."

Zao's jaw drops. "What? How is that possible? Do you know how many powerful people would kill in order to receive that knowledge?"

"I know. Starskin is the key to surviving the interdimensional rifts. But sometimes the *Starglider*s become warped in the voyage. The *Starglider* Ser Kodak used to transport the other Abels became warped and unusable. They had to construct another one to travel back home. The final Abel I tracked down was salvaging material in order to return home."

"Which was in—"

"Aegis 12, yes."

"Wow." Zao leans back in his copilot seat, the information visibly racing through his mind, as he processes this new revelation. "Or an Abel," he spurts, "This is crazy, multiple universes? Do you think that is what Cyra and this Keeper are trying to accomplish?"

Abel brings his bruised hand to his chin. "It's extremely likely."

"And do you know who this Keeper is?"

Abel shakes his head. "That is a variable I don't know. A man who studied Kodak's work, perhaps? Whoever he is, he's powerful and has enough resources to pursue this goal and hire an army if he needs to. Not to mention Cyra is working with him. They're both people we can't underestimate."

"No shit," Zao says. "I've reached out to all of my contacts, including some people with high status in the underworld. Absolutely nobody has heard of this guy. The man's a ghost. Anyone who can acquire resources and influence without being a blip on anyone's radar is someone we should be worried about."

"Agreed." Abel nods, the gears turning in his mind.

"So," Zao continues. "How do we take this guy down?"

Abel locks eyes with Zao. "Very carefully and skillfully."

Zao chuckles softly. "No offense, friend, but I saw you with Cyra, and you ain't got much in that department."

Abel raises his arms in defense. "Hey, I'm a Collector, not a soldier."

"Well, it wouldn't hurt to take a few boxing classes,"

Zao remarks. "Anyway, looks like we're coming up to Loberon's orbit."

Abel and Zao set up to brace themselves, as the countdown on the monitor blips in red numbers. Three... Two... One.

With a loud crack and a flash of light, *The Tip of the Spear* halts above orbit around Loberon. The icy planet takes up most of their view from the cockpit, and Station 17 can be seen as Loberon's moon shines above them. The ship traffic between the planet and the space station is still busy in the freighter line, almost as if nothing has changed since their departure.

Cleo hooks herself in her kiosk in the ship, her hologram on the cockpit's dashboard. Cleo transforms into an owl, a fitting animal to scan the scene for prey in a field.

"All right, Cleo." Abel taps the monitor screen. "Let's give this a shot. Scan the general frequencies for any traffic that simulate code patterns. Flag anything that may be secret communications."

A few moments pass as Cleo's holographic owl darts its head back and forth, scanning the scene. Different broadcasting channels can be heard as Cleo works. Abel and Zao listen to Cleo zoom through channels between freighters, music stations, and news stations that are reporting about the Satyr Militia compound raid.

Finally, Cleo stops on a music station. The radio is playing a static-heavy song, an old one but familiar, but static stops the song between lyrics.

Take me home... *static*

Country *Static* roads...

To the place... *static* *static*

"It's just an old radio station." Zao shrugs.

"No, listen." Abel leans his ear closer to the monitor. Then he hears it clearly. "It's not the lyrics…it's the static. There's a pattern, it's Morse code."

"How in the—"

"Cleo, count the static breaks in this song and apply it to a Morse code translation. Let's see what it says."

A few more moments pass until Cleo displays a message on the monitor in bright red letters:

Regroup. SM.

A series of numbers follow the message.

"Coordinates," Zao says. "Think it's them?"

"Let's see." Abel sets his hands on the yoke of the ship. "Cleo, route those coordinates."

A few seconds pass, and Cleo marks the location on the navigational computer—a location still in the Sovlikian system.

Abel shrugs. "I mean, I've pursued leads with less info than this."

"What if it isn't them?" Zao asks.

"Well 'SM' in the message gives me confidence, but if it isn't them, we'll have to warp to Promethium and figure this out. We don't have enough time to chase help."

Zao sighs loudly. "In that case, let's do it."

Abel nods and flips some switches on the dashboard. "Cleo, initiate the pulse engines in three… two… one."

The Tip of the Spear jolts forward with the fury of an arrow. The stars surrounding them turn into cosmic rays, and the universe flies by like dust in the wind.

Chapter 20

In the vast, cold space lies debris of dead ships floating aimlessly among the stars. Once proud ships, their crews ranged from a couple members to hundreds. Now they join another graveyard. Among the wretched, floating debris, a flash of light erupts in the distance with a loud crack. *The Tip of the Spear* flashes into the field of dead ships.

Abel flips on the headlights and analyzes the wreckages floating around them. Meanwhile, Zao gawks at the bits of metal and rubber. Cargo containers, furniture, and various scraps float by their cockpit window.

"Well, I for one regret coming here," Zao remarks.

"They have to be around here somewhere," Abel suggests.

"How? Where can people meet up around this boneyard?"

"Perhaps in an intact ship?"

"Doubt it."

Abel pushes the yoke, and the vessel jolts forward. Gently passing the debris, they hear loud booms of the scrap colliding with the outside of the hull. The ship is a tough ship, but Abel still proceeds with caution.

"Maybe all the Satyrs have moved on," Zao suggests.

"You know, for someone who is in the Collector business, you're awfully doubtful," Abel remarks as he focuses his attention on flying. "Cleo, give us a quick scan."

The holographic owl spreads its wings, and a visible scan is sent out through the debris field, reflecting off the scrap metal.

Abel studies the monitor after the initial scan and turns it so Zao can read it. "See, we got live bodies around here, as well as a ship signature."

"Well, I'll be damned," Zao mumbles.

Abel gently twists the yoke, and the ship slowly moves toward the source. Passing by debris and wreckage, the ship's headlights reflect off the scrap metal as it slices through the darkness like a knife. *Good thing I'm not concerned with the paint job.*

A few moments pass until Abel and Zao arrive at the source of the signatures, then they see it. A mid-sized freighter, meandering among the scrap. The freighter shows exterior damage with no signs of it being operational. Abel leans forward. It's not a combat freighter of any kind; rather it seems industrial. It also looks old, as if grounded by the industrial company it served years ago.

"This is the source?" Zao asks, fixated on the dark freighter.

"Seems like it," Abel replies.

"It doesn't appear functional. Are you sure Vadim and his people are on there?"

"It looks mostly intact. The lights are off, but that doesn't mean nobody is home."

Zao sighs. He studies the dormant freighter for a few moments longer. "I don't see any sign of life."

"Look," Abel says, "We came all this way. We might as well go inside." He pushes the throttle and manipulates the vessel to proceed slowly. The ship approaches the freighter so they can examine the hull with the ship's headlights. *The Tip of the Spear* hums, hovering close to the freighter as it looks for an opening. Then they stumble upon the hangar doors on the side of the ship, closed as tight as a can.

"Hm." Abel presses his lips together, staring at the hangar doors. "This seems to be the way in, but how to open it?"

"Maybe give Cleo a shot at finding out?" Zao suggests. "I wouldn't expect the Satyr Militia to leave the door unlocked."

"All right. Cleo, give it a quick scan."

Cleo's holographic owl spreads its wings again and scans the entirety of the ship. The resulting data is then darted back into the monitor in the cockpit, and Abel examines the newly gathered info.

"Cleo is saying that the ship is in lockdown, but the emergency power is on. That means the life support is still functioning." Abel reads the data out loud.

"Cleo, can you uplift the lockdown?" Zao asks.

Cleo gives an affirming beep, and the holographic owl's head spins around and around. Zao gasps at the turning owl head, then off in the distance, a light above the hangar doors illuminates, and it rotates and flashes. The doors part slightly with a jolt, then slowly opens.

"Open sesame," Abel mumbles and pushes on the throttle to dock the ship inside the freighter. He lands inside the hangar, and the headlights from the ship light up the interior. The hangar doors close behind them, and darkness engulfs the ship. Abel and Zao wait for the hangar to seal and depressurize. Once they are confident it's safe to leave the ship, they unclick their seatbelts and move to the boarding ramp.

"Remember," Abel starts. "These guys may be jumpy. They're not expecting us, so we play it nice and cool and make no sudden movements."

Zao raises his hand in reassurance. "Relax, we sold guns to these guys. I know how jumpy they can be."

Abel slams his fist on the boarding ramp controls, and the ramp jolts open and sets down on the metallic floor of the hangar. "Yeah, and let's not get shot by those guns, okay?" Abel turns his attention away from Zao and looks forward.

A line of militants point those same guns at him and Zao.

Abel can't see the faces of the militants, since each rifle pointed at them shines a bright light in his face. He squints, searching for Vadim, and Zao raises his hands above his head.

The room is eerily silent until one voice erupts from the squad, "State your business or we end you right here and now."

Abel lifts his hands above his head. "Easy now. We're just looking for Vadim."

"How did you find us?" The voice demands.

"We listened to your song, 'Country roads'?" Abel shrugs and cuts a sideways glimpse at Zao, who is sweating profusely.

"What is going on?" A thick Sovlikian accent booms from behind the wall of lights—an accent Abel immediately recognizes.

The other voice replies to the man, "They say they are looking for you, and they found us somehow from a song."

"Let me see," The Sovlikian voice replies, yet Abel doesn't see any movement. "I know them. Everyone lower your weapons."

The lights shine away from their faces, now illuminating the militants standing before them. They show signs of starvation and exhaustion, and many smell as if they haven't taken a shower for days. Vadim emerges from the bundle of militants, his mechanical eye shining in the darkness.

"How did you get here?" Vadim asks.

"We cracked your code," Zao speaks up. "We've been looking for you."

"Why?" Vadim demands, weariness apparent in his voice.

"It's Eva," Abel replies. "She's been taken."

"Taken? How?"

Abel and Zao exchange looks, then Abel addresses Vadim, "She was taken by a shadow group. We need your help to get her back."

Vadim stares at the two of them, then waves them down. "Come with me to the bridge. Tell me everything on the way."

***

Vadim leads Abel and Zao to the bridge, with Cleo trailing behind in her owl form. Satyr operatives perform different duties. All look exhausted, and the tension is palpable on the bridge.

"You're telling me that this 'Keeper' now has Eva and is threatening to kill her if you don't turn yourself over to him?"

"Yes," Abel replies.

"Why does he want you?"

"I know something that he doesn't, and he needs it to fulfill his agenda."

Vadim then stops and turns to Abel. "Why didn't you do it then if you care for Eva's safe return?"

Abel steps closer to Vadim to deliver his point. "What you need to know is that if this Keeper gets the information he needs, he'll wipe out worlds and disrupt solar systems. You think the Federation industrial economy is destructive? This man wants to destroy solar systems for the sake of science."

Vadim is silent for a moment, yet he doesn't break his intimidating gaze from Abel. "How do I know this isn't bullshit?"

"Because Eva is taken, and I know your group cares for her," Abel whispers. "You don't have to believe this story about the destruction of worlds, but you need to believe that Eva is in danger."

"Hm." Vadim sets his chin in his hand, then turns to both Abel and Zao. "What exactly do you need from us?"

Zao steps forward. "We need armed help. This man has mercenaries under his payroll, well-trained ones for that matter. Abel and I can't just show up alone."

"You're expecting heavy resistance?" Vadim asks.

"We're expecting anything," Abel remarks. "These people are powerful, dedicated, and unpredictable. We encountered them on Uvir, and they're dangerous."

"Uvir? What were you doing on Uvir?"

"Looking for warp fuel," Zao chimes in. "Eva suggested the old Satyr outpost to salvage fuel, since the Federation had their ports on lockdown. They intercepted us there."

"And that is where they took Eva," Abel adds.

Vadim frowns and is quiet for a few moments, then he peers up. "Do you know where they are?"

"Promethium," Abel answers. "Do you have any warp fuel to get there?"

Vadim shakes his head. "The Federation is starving us, which is why we're here. This ship will hopefully last us until we find a source. Yet, things are looking slim."

"We have warp fuel," Abel states. "Vadim, if you decide to help us, we'll have enough room for a team. You guys are all we got, all that Eva's got. If you don't help us, Zao and I will be forced to go straight there, and Eva may not have a chance."

"Hm." Vadim appears to be thinking. Then his voice booms and echoes through the bridge. "Ivan!"

A young man answers from the platform above them, "Yes, sir?"

"How fast can you assemble a fire team, and how many?"

"I can gather a small team of five."

"Make that six." Vadim cracks his knuckles, then his neck. "I am coming with you. Assemble the team, Ivan. Get them equipped ASAP."

"Yes sir." Ivan bolts toward the doors of the bridge. Then Abel turns toward Vadim. "Thank you."

"Thank me when Eva is safe with us." Vadim follows Ivan's path out the door and waves Abel and Zao to follow. "We need to arm ourselves and form a plan."

Chapter 21

The Keeper stands in his stone courtyard, gazing into the sky with his hands interlocked behind his back, the moonlight reflecting off his face, his mask in his hands. The peaceful sounds of Promethium echoes through the courtyard. That is, until the mercenary ship flies overhead and lands on the other side of the estate.

After the sounds of the engines whir down, footsteps echo from the stone, the familiar rhythm of Cyra's walk. He turns to face her, expecting news. She stops before him, her hands at her sides, her posture straight. "The replacements have arrived, as you requested."

"Yes, they were sure to interrupt my peace," The Keeper snarls. "What of Servant?"

"Servant is nearly repaired, with a security upgrade to prevent another unforeseen breach."

"Good." The Keeper turns back, scanning the surroundings.

"Eva is secured in the estate, ready to make the exchange whenever Abel arrives. Which I don't understand. Why hire the extra help if it's only going to be a damaged Collector and a fat man?"

"Because you kidnapped a former member of the Satyr Militia." The Keeper turns around, his voice intensifying. "I don't think you remember. This is a man who killed many people, including your grandfather, to prevent this goal. He's also smart enough to know we are expecting him, and he still wants to prevent us from achieving this goal. Meaning he is going to bring help, most likely Eva's old associates."

Cyra bites her lip, meeting The Keeper's gaze with equal anger. "Oh, I remember clearly."

"Good. Don't get too emotional, Cyra. Remember our mission."

Cyra almost snarls as she turns to leave, "I'll address our new contractors."

"That would be best," The Keeper replies. After she leaves, he gazes down at his black mask, seeing his image in its glossy surface. "Soon, I'll be home."

***

A loud crack rings throughout the empty space above Promethium along with a flash of light. *The Tip of the Spear* finishes its warp to the system, followed by silence. From the ship's cockpit, the whole planet can be seen. Abel, Zao, and Vadim bask in its beauty.

"So, this is Promethium," Zao observes. "It's—wow!"

"This is what we fight to protect," Vadim says, his eyes gazing at the panoramic vista.

"Yeah, this is where my collecting career began." Abel says. "Eva is down there. Along with our enemy. They're most likely expecting us."

"Where are they held?" Vadim asks.

Abel checks his monitor. "Cleo." A hologram of Cleo's

owl erects on the dashboard, awaiting orders. "Give the surface a quick scan and locate any man-made structures."

Cleo gives an affirming beep and spreads its spectral wings to send out a scan. A few seconds pass, and the data becomes visible on the monitor, which displays a replica of the planet. Cleo then blips a red dot on the map.

"Wow, only one structure." Zao remarks. "You would think more people would live here."

"At least it won't be an issue figuring out where they are," Abel states and unclicks his seatbelt. "We need a plan before we go down there. C'mon."

Abel heads to the center hub of the ship while it floats in orbit. Zao and Vadim follow. Voices coming from the hub inform Abel they're not the first to arrive. As they enter the room, all the Satyr militants stand in attention.

"All right, here's the situation," Abel addresses the group. "We know the location where Eva is most likely being held. Trouble is, we don't know exactly what we're dealing with, and we don't know how many armed contractors they have there."

Vadim steps forward to address Abel. "You've been on this planet before. What exactly can you tell us?"

Abel looks down at the center-hub table. "Cleo, display the map."

A holographic map appears on the center table, showing spectral mountains and valleys. A red outline of a building is shown on top of a cliff, as well as red outlines underneath the building all leading to a large space.

"Is that an estate?" Vadim asks.

"It would seem that The Keeper is the luxurious type," Zao adds. "What is this down here?" He asks while pointing to the large space underneath the estate.

Abel peers closer at the large space. "I don't know. It could be a storage facility or a lab."

"Or a hangar." Vadim cuts in. "See how the space is close to the cliff face. It could be storing a ship—a large one, it appears."

"There are various landing platforms around the estate." Abel points to several spots on the map. "Most likely for his mercs and other pawns. A couple of other ships are parked around the estate, yet nothing that I can see down in the hangar or facility down below."

"I'll send a recon team down to the surface." Vadim points to a couple of Satyr militants. "You and you will go down and—"

"No," Abel cuts him off.

"No?"

"We can't risk them being caught. If your guys get detected, The Keeper will kill Eva."

"We don't know what we're dealing with," Vadim retorts. "My men are more than capable."

"I don't doubt your men, Vadim. But these people most likely have the entire planet under surveillance."

"Then what do you suggest?" Vadim crosses his arms.

Abel sets his hands on the counter, his lips pressed together. How to proceed? If The Keeper detects them-- anyone other than himself—he'll kill Eva or move her. He still needs Abel, and in reality, killing Eva will not give The Keeper much leverage. But Abel can't risk it.

Abel faces everyone waiting for his reply. "Okay, here's what we're going to do."

Chapter 22

Eva can't help but rock in her given room. The white walls surrounding is suffocating. The bed is too soft, the room is too clean, and the guard standing post outside makes her uneasy. She wants to cover the walls with drawings and loose paper, like a bite that can't be scratched. They made sure she didn't have any way to write, so she pulls her hair and bites her nails, anything to cope with the quiet. As the hours drag on, it's becoming a losing battle.

They're not coming.
They're not coming.
They're not coming.

The whispers in Eva's mind become more intense with each passing hour. With nothing to keep her busy, nothing for her to keep her hands moving, no one to talk to, her mind takes over. Desperation sets in, a madness crawling into her skin.

That is, until the doorknob turns.

Cyra stands in the doorway with a mercenary behind her. Her face shows no emotion, and she wears fatigues with a sleeveless shirt. Her arms now bask in a waving glow, as if the sunset is absorbed into her metallic arms. She is no longer hiding, confident and impervious. "Come on. It's showtime."

Eva stands with difficulty, her back sore and her tailbone stiff from rocking back and forth for hours. With arms wrapped around her waist, she approaches Cyra. "What...what is going on?" Eva asks with a soft yet trembling voice.

"Follow me." Cyra turns and heads down the hallway without batting Eva an eye. Eva glances behind her and finds the mercenary holding his plasma repeater, his black glossy helmet reflecting Eva's face.

They walk through the estate to the entrance. Mercenaries march in groups around the estate, armed to the teeth. Something is going on, and her spirit seems to be lifting.

Perhaps they've come after all.

Cyra leads Eva to the entrance, and they stop at the top of the stairs leading to the large marble columns. A couple of contractors stand post by the front door, and the large droid, known as Servant, towers over the steps. They move forward, then Eva sees someone standing alone by the landing pad.

Abel. No one else. Only Abel. No Zao, no Cleo, no *Tip of the Spear*. Abel stands there in his usual coat, emitting whiffs of familiar odors in the gentle winds of Promethium.

"So," Cyra exclaims from the top of the steps. "Finally made up your mind?"

Abel shrugs in an oddly relaxed behavior. "I figured the only way to end this and ensure Eva is safe is to give myself up."

***

Cyra's head tilts to the side. She hoped Abel would attempt to rescue Eva in a more theatrical sense. "Where is your monk friend?"

"Oh, him? He bailed once he knew the true risks," Abel replies. "You really shook him up back on Uvir."

Cyra's body remains still, and the mercenaries scan the scene around Abel. She doesn't have a good feeling about Abel just giving himself up. She announces from the top of the stairs. "You know the deal. Come up, and we'll set Eva free."

Abel raises his hand, and the two mercenaries raise their rifles in response. "Before that, I wanna see him."

"See whom?" Cyra asks back.

"The Keeper. Your employer."

For the next few moments, the only sounds are the gentle wind and the rustling trees. Cyra locks eyes with Abel, both remaining as calm as the wind.

"Why?" Cyra asks. "You will see him soon enough."

"I guess I'm curious."

With a scowl, Cyra pulls out a plasma pistol and points the muzzle at Eva's head. The quick, sudden motion causes Eva's knees to buckle.

"May I add another suggestion?" Cyra says. "I will give you ten seconds to get up here, or I scatter her brains and paint this marble red. Then I'll send our faithful employees to retrieve you and drag you back in as many pieces as possible without killing you."

The wind picks up pace, and lines frame Abel's mouth. He raises his hands and moves forward. "Easy now, easy. No need to start counting. I'm coming up."

Cyra's snarled lip turns into a smile. Abel climbs the

marble stairs, and Eva stands at the top, still as the marble surrounding them. Finally, Abel stands before them with both arms raised.

"All right, Cyra. Let her go," Abel demands.

Cyra stares at Abel for a moment, then lowers her pistol. "Go," She tells Eva without breaking eye contact with Abel.

***

Eva sends a worried glance at Abel, her eyes wide from the adrenaline racing through her body. Abel only nods at her. Not a word, not even a whisper. Ill at ease, she starts down the steps, glancing back toward Abel, whom they escort inside the estate, and whose arms slowly lower from above his head.

Eva wants to cry. Her eyes well, yet no tears come out. She stands on the other side of the landing pad in front of the estate, waiting for any noises or alarms to give her a reason to run back inside. She doesn't want to leave him, not after everything that she has learned. Not after learning the true identity of The Keeper.

She continues stepping backwards, not breaking sight of the estate. When she reaches the tree line, large hands emerge from the brush and grab her, swallowing her into the vegetation. Eva would've screamed if it wasn't for the meaty hand covering her mouth. A man's voice shushes in her ear, and his foul breath makes her wince.

"Easy, Eva, it's all okay."

Recognizing the thick accent, her body slumps into his arms, and her muscles go limp. He uncovers her mouth and lets her loose.

"Vadim?" Eva whispers.

Vadim nods, smiling as a few more Satyr militants kneel behind him. They stay concealed in the brush, their eyes fixated on the guards rotating shifts at the estate.

"What are you doing here?" Eva asks.

"Abel brought us. Said he needed help saving you and stopping this Keeper. Who is he?"

Eva is silent, Vadim won't believe what she says about The Keeper, so she tells the short version of the truth. "He's a powerful man—someone who is trying to finalize this experiment. He is willing to destroy worlds to do it."

The Satyrs exchange looks. "We need to save Abel. We can't just leave him," Eva whispers. She stares at the estate, looking for any sign that Abel is okay.

"You don't need to worry, Eva." A familiar voice speaks from behind her.

She whirls around. Abel has joined the group. Before Abel can say another word, Eva wraps her arms around him.

***

The quick and quiet embrace leaves Abel stunned, and his arms pinned to his side. Eva steps back, and he clears his throat. "Are you okay?" Abel asks her.

"Yes, Abel. That man—"

"Don't worry, Eva." Abel cuts her off then turns to Vadim. "Did they take it?"

"Yes," Vadim replies. "It would seem that Cleo is now a guest of The Keeper's manor."

"Good." Abel kneels next to Eva. "Did they hurt you at all or—?"

"No." She shakes her head. "The Keeper told me his plan."

"Who is he?" Vadim asks.

Eva turns to Vadim and the other Satyrs. "His name is Kane. A man who has built this experiment for years and built his wealth to do it." She pulls Abel to the side, addressing him in a hushed voice, "The Keeper told me his plan for the experiment. He has one."

"He has what?" Abel whispers back.

"A *Starglider,* a complete and functional *Starglider.*"

Abel falls silent and presses his lips together. "He's close then. All he needs is the map, then he'll be off to a star that will be ample room to open a gate."

"Once he finds out that you're not actually there, then—"

"He's going to send everything after us. Even if we leave now, he won't stop until he has me. We have to end him here, now."

"So how do we do that?" Eva asks.

Abel turns to Vadim and his men. "Vadim, how much longer until dark?"

Vadim checks the data pad on his wrist. "About a half hour. Once darkness falls, we will strike." Vadim then presses against his ear and speaks through his comms. "Assault team Bravo, are you in position? Over."

Abel hears the comms through his own earpiece, interspersed with static. Then a voice cuts through. "Affirmative, we are in position, Zulu, awaiting attack order. Currently, we have a squad of hostiles guarding this entrance. Over."

"Affirmative Bravo, wait for contact to be initiated from our front, then commence the assault. Over." Vadim drops his hand from his ear and nods to Abel and Eva. "They're in position."

"Good." Abel turns to Eva. "You're going back to the ship."

"Wait, what?"

"Zao is there, and he is playing surveillance. You will

be—"

"The hell I'm going with Zao." Eva straightens.

"This is what we're doing, Eva." Abel retorts, his voice firm and cold. The setting sun highlights the craters of his blister scars—he can feel the sun's heat on them. "This is my burden, not yours. We're ending this, and you're going to be with Zao away from the gunfire."

Eva is silent. She kneels on the soft ground with her arms wrapped around herself and stares back at Abel.

"One of our squad mates will escort you," Vadim interjects. "You must go now. The sun is setting."

Eva casts one last glance at Abel. "Be careful." Then she follows the Satyr militant through the bush.

"Your burden?" Vadim turns to Abel as they wait for the sun to go down.

"It started here, with me. I tried to stop it and run away from it, but I should've known that these people wouldn't stop."

"A man this dangerous is everyone's burden and responsibility to stop. When you talk about the destruction of worlds and lives, it's no longer just your fight."

Abel slowly turns his head toward Vadim. He's never thought of it that way. The moment when he saw his colleagues and Ethan die in the cavern with the obelisk, and the moment Ser Kodak gunned down the rest of the Collectors, he always thought that he was alone. When his home was swallowed by the void, and everything he knew was gone, he shouldered that burden all by himself. Simply because he knew no other way.

Yet, when he found his own grim reminder of mortality, it sent him on a search for answers that he had erased in the past. Abel has rallied these people along the way, all here now, their weapons drawn toward the estate owned by a man as insane as Ser Kodak.

The sun finally sets, and darkness falls. The familiar dancing lights return to the sky, and the Armageddon of the moon shines brightly despite its destruction. He looks toward the estate and raises the plasma repeater in his hands. The emergence of the dark beauty of Promethium's night means that blood will be shed.

He started this fight alone. Now he will end it with allies.

Chapter 23

Cyra ushers Abel into the estate, making sure that he is escorted inside by the armed mercenaries. Before heading inside, she peers at Promethium's sunset, basking in its beauty for a moment. She wishes there were more of these moments to soak in the rays of the lowering sun. Perhaps when this is over, she'll have the freedom to indulge herself.

"Madam Kodak?" A mercenary's distorted voice interrupts her thoughts.

"Yes, I'm behind you," she replies.

The mercenary heads inside. She takes one last look at the sun. It's going to be dark soon. Better get on with it. There is something odd about this man named Abel, yet Cyra can't place her finger on it. This is way too easy. Why did he give himself up?

Abel stands between the mercenaries, remaining silent, but his appraising eyes dart around the estate.

"I didn't figure you to be the surrendering type," Cyra addresses him when they arrive in the common area. "Did you have a change of heart? Or perhaps you do care for that girl?"

She locks eyes with Abel, tilting her head, waiting for a response. After a few seconds of silence, Abel shrugs.

How unusual. Cyra steps forward to study Abel's face. His eyes follow hers, yet his face is still, completely lacking in emotion. Finally, her patience with diplomacy grows thin. She grabs him by the coat. "The Keeper will sure love to—" The moment her hand contacts Abel's collar, it passes through his body like a cloud. Everyone, including Cyra, gasps. The mercenaries jump back and point their rifles at Abel; others point their weapons at the windows.

Abel's body then transforms, its particles morphing into a new shape. His color changes into a shade of sapphire blue, his arms become wings and his legs become talons. From a man to a spectral hawk in front of her eyes.

Cleo.

Before she knows it, Cleo passes through a window, the glass shatters in her wake, and the spectral hawk takes flight into Promethium's night sky.

Cyra peers around. What just happened? Then she looks out the window. The darkness of the night has fallen, their trick to get Eva back to safely and out of her grasp has worked, and the diversion to throw them off guard has trumped her plan. Then she remembers.

Abel is not the surrendering type.

Time has slowed down, and her own heartbeat resounds through her ears. Before another thought passes her mind, she grabs a thick, oak table and flips it over for cover. Once she kneels behind it, all hell breaks loose.

Plasma fire rips through the windows and mercenaries stand in the way. The sudden plasma fire erupts the estate in a display of blood and chaos. Glass fragments and wooden splinters, along with marble dust and plasma smoke, fill the air of the common area in an instant. Cyra covers her head with her arms, and she hears the sudden cries of pain and the commands of the mercenaries, their voices modulated through their helmets.

A few of the mercenaries fall to the ground, the sound of choking from inside their helmets. Others rush to cover and return fire. Peeking around cover, their weapons flash in the darkness.

One runs to Cyra's cover and checks on her. She swats him away and grabs the pistol from her belt. Peeking over the table, Cyra finds the common area littered with debris and blood. She scans past the open front doors to see flashes coming from the tree line. Cyra fires in the direction of the flashes, hoping to see some results of her shot placement.

The mercenary next to Cyra fires relentlessly, switching between targets. The other mercenaries change covers, yelling instructions to their cohorts, yet they're firing into the dark. In a flash, plasma fire erupts from the side windows, shattering the glass. A couple of mercenaries take the blow, red mist exploding from their bodies. They fall to the floor.

Cyra knows that the enemy has the advantage up here, despite the estate's marble structure. They can see her, yet she can't see them. Not through all of the plasma smoke and flashes.

"Everyone fall back," she yells through the chaos. "Fall back into the estate."

The mercenaries obey. They backpedal, while returning fire through the windows. Switching between targets and firing in the general direction of the plasma fire, a mercenary catches a blast in the neck and presses his hand against the squirting wound as his squad mate helps him retreat.

The plasma fire continues for a few more seconds, then ceases. The common area is almost completely destroyed. Burns and holes have torn through the doors, the windows are shattered, and the furniture is strewn everywhere. Mercenaries lay lifeless on the ground, their blood pooling on the marble and rugs.

***

Lights peer through the windows and doorways, and Abel and Vadim move into the common area, their weapons at the ready.

The Satyr militants follow. Some have scrapes and wounds from the mercenaries returning fire, but no casualties. They move with their rifles pointing at corners and check the bodies. Remaining silent, they tread carefully, avoiding tripping over bodies and debris. Abel examines the bodies, searching for a familiar face. Yet he finds none and concludes that Cyra survived and retreated further into the estate.

Cyra and this Kane must be waiting inside. Abel scans the room, looking for any possible escape routes. The inside of this estate is massive.

"Abel," Vadim calls out in a whisper. "This way."

He stands next to a doorway with some of the militants. Abel joins the group and nods to Vadim, who inches open the door, and they advance inside.

Once they enter, they gasp at what they find—a large room filled with art, marble sculptures, and a large windowed wall illuminated by moonlight. Abel scans the gallery, looking for anyone who may be a target, yet he finds none.

"What is this?" Vadim asks, surveying the gallery.

Abel recognizes some of the art pieces and the general taste of the gallery. "It's Ser Kodak's art collection."

"The man had taste for sure," Vadim says, his voice filled with awe.

"We have to stay focused. They're still around here somewhere," Abel says.

"Right." Vadim points to the rest of the Satyr militants. "You, you, you, and you. Form up and investigate the rest of the estate. You stay with Abel and me. Split up and cover more ground."

They salute, and four of the militants form a line and depart the gallery. The remaining militant stays close to Abel and Vadim.

Static pierces Abel's ear, then a familiar voice.

"Abel, do you copy? It's Zao, over."

"I copy," Abel replies with his hand pressed against the earpiece.

"Eva just arrived on the ship. What's going on?"

"We're in the estate now. This place is enormous."

"Yeah, I see that. We're circling the estate with the ship. Everything's quiet from up here."

"Okay, good. Keep an eye out for—" Abel tries to reply, then screams resound behind him, then silence. Abel and Vadim spin to find the Satyr militant with them being held in the air by a large droid. With a loud snap, the militant's body hangs lifeless.

Servant approaches them with loud steps, then drops the militant.

"Abel? Abel are you there?" Zao calls through the radio channel.

"We'll call you back, Zao." Abel replies, and raises his

rifle, as does Vadim. Both of their rifles flash fire at Servant, their tri-barrels rotating rapidly, and the smoke from the muzzles rising in the air.

Servant marches on and shakes off the plasma burns with the back of his hand.

"Please do not resist." Its cold, robotic voice sends chills down their spines.

Abel and Vadim backstep, continuing to fire. Yet the plasma pings smoke off of the droid's metal skin. Its red eyes glow brightly in the darkness.

"This isn't working," Vadim exclaims as his rifle overheats in his hand.

"Spread out and don't let it get close," Abel shouts back. Vadim nods and heads in the opposite direction of Abel, causing Servant to look back and forth trying to pick a victim. Then, Servant locks its gaze on Vadim.

"C'mon, you abomination." Vadim taunts the large droid, and Abel searches for an opening while it's distracted.

As Abel raises his rifle and points it at the droid's back, a hand reaches out from the shadows and grabs his rifle.

He whirls to find Cyra tossing his rifle out of reach. As quick as it happened, Cyra's fist plows into his gut. Abel's feet leave the ground and his body flies through the air. His torso slams into a painting and falls face-first onto the ground. The wind escapes his lungs, and he coughs onto the hardwood floor, forming a pool of saliva and drops of blood. *Blood... Damn.*

He raises his head, but his vision blurs from the impact, yet the shape of Cyra approaches him. Vadim is still backpedaling and firing at Servant, an unstoppable force of machination.

Abel presses his finger to his earpiece and gurgles into

it. "This is Abel. We need assistance now in the gallery." He coughs between the words and feels air returning to his lungs. Glancing up, Cyra, in a flash of reflective light, slams her fist down upon him. Somehow, he rolls out of the way of her blow, and the hardwood floor splinters and shatters where he lay.

Cyra's eyes are frantic with hate as Abel evades her blow. She growls and clenches her fist, then bolts toward Abel as he holds his hand to his gut. His eyes dart for his rifle or any weapon. Just like on Uvir, he scrambles to evade from Cyra, hunting for a means to defend himself.

Then the rapid firing of Vadim's plasma rifle stop, followed by a grunt as Vadim is tossed across the gallery. The comms in Abel's ear are full of frantic voices and commands, while plasma fire erupts amongst the static. The other Satyr militants must be fighting the rest of the mercenaries.

"Abel?" Zao's voice in the comms. "What's going on?"

Abel presses his finger against his earpiece. "Vadim and I are in the gallery, and Cyra is kicking my ass again," he replies, grunting in pain.

"The gallery?" Eva's voice rings through the comms. "The room with the large, moon-lit window and all of the art?"

"Yeah, why?"

A brief pause passes through the radio channel, and then Eva speaks up again, "Get her to stand in the center of the gallery."

"Why?"

"Just do it."

The command from Eva causes Abel to wince. He glances at Vadim who nods. Abel pivots to face Cyra. At the same time, Vadim focus on Servant, shouting insults at the droid.

Abel's eyes clash with Cyra's, and he lifts his hands in a taunting fashion. "You know—" he begins. "No matter what you accomplish here, no matter how many breakthroughs you make, no matter how many gates you open, even killing me, you'll never make your old man proud."

The words cause Cyra to bare her teeth and clench her fist. Abel casts a sideways glance at Vadim, who's leading Servant to the center of the gallery. His turn.

"You think he would ever be proud of you? Puleez. Even with your Starskin arms and the progress you've made with his legacy, you're just a pretty girl in his eyes."

"You don't know anything," she snarls. "You think because you have the knowledge of an ancient race printed in your head, you're special. I'm the one that continued his mission. And I'm the one who built on his legacy, rather than destroy it like you." She's reached the center of the gallery unawares, caught in the heat of the moment.

"I am the one who will be remembered," She yells, angry tears brimming in her eyes.

Abel then catches something bright in the corner of his eye. Headlights of a ship quickly approaching the window like a meteor falling from the night sky. Yet he remains focused on Cyra. "Is that right? Well, he certainly didn't remember you."

Cyra cringes at his last words. The glass wall of the gallery shatters as *The Tip of the Spear* pierces through. Like a loud clap of thunder, the ship flies into the gallery in a massive display of chaos and destruction. Servant is the first to catch the wrath of the vessel as Vadim rolls out of the way. Then Cyra's eyes widen at the ship barreling toward her. The floor craters, and the room shakes violently. Abel's ears deafen from the crash, and Vadim holds his ears. Flying debris makes Abel shield his face.

As soon as it happens, the gallery becomes quiet. Abel uncovers his face. A bright red streak remains where Cyra was standing. His prized ship now leans against the *Der Krieg* painting, and the bay door opens from the rear. Vadim pushes himself up, opening his mouth to unblock his ears.

Eva and Zao climb out of the rear of the ship. They look dazed, and Abel slowly approaches them with his arms raised in disbelief. "Why my ship?" Abel surveys the wreckage, shaking his head slowly.

"Well," Zao shrugs. "Your ship didn't have cannons mounted so—"

The trio share a moment of silence. Then Eva chuckles, and Zao joins her. After a moment, the chuckles turn into roaring laughter.

"You're paying the bill for that," Abel states coldly.

"I know, I know." Zao clears his throat.

Vadim joins the group. He stands with his hands on his knees and takes a deep breath. "That was perhaps the most reckless flying I have ever seen."

The comms rings through everyone's ears, and a Satyr militant speaks. "I think that's the last of them. We've suffered a couple of casualties. Is everyone else good in the gallery? We heard a loud crash."

Vadim presses a finger to his ear. "We're fine. Lost one. Gallery secured," he replies with labored breaths.

Eva clears her throat. "That only leaves Kane."

"Where would he be?" Zao asks. "Has he been hiding this whole time?"

"I bet he's in the hangar," Eva suggests.

"Is that where the *Starglider* is stored?" Abel asks.

Eva nods.

"Okay." Abel sighs deeply. The endeavor of this day rests heavy on his shoulders. He is so close. He must finish it, so he musters the will to press forward and turns to address his companions. "All of you, thank you. For everything. I have never faced any challenges with allies. With friends."

Vadim, Eva, and Zao grin.

"But what comes next, I must do alone. I must deal with Kane." Abel expects cries of protests, but to his surprise, he receives none. Zao nods, and Eva hugs herself. Vadim steps forward and sets his greasy hand on Abel's shoulder.

"I'll gather the squad and wait outside," Vadim says. "We'll keep an eye on the sky just in case he takes off."

Abel nods. Eva picks up Cyra's plasma pistol off the pool of blood and hands it to Abel. Abel wipes the blood off the handle and grips it firmly in his hand.

"Be careful," Eva says softly. With that, the group leaves the destroyed gallery. Abel makes sure they pass through the doors safely. Once they're out of his sight, he scans the gallery one last time. All of this wealth and luxury destroyed in a matter of an hour. He spots a set of doors that should lead to the hangar.

Abel sets his hands on the cold oak door with a deep sigh, taking a moment for himself, gathering the strength for what comes next. All this way, all this pain, all this burden are about to end. Whatever comes, bring it on.

With that, he pushes the doors wide open.

Chapter 24

The hinges creak against the heavy weight of the door. Abel scans the massive hangar and can't believe his eyes.

Just like what he found on Aegis 12, rather than a wreckage, a vessel lies in the middle of the hangar. About twice the size of *The Tip of the Spear*, the vessel's hull displays hinted waves of light rippling through the surface. The hazy gold almost blinds him, and the solar sails spread out like wings. He stares at it with his mouth agape.

It is not every day that one witnesses a *Starglider* with their own eyes, let alone one that's intact. Abel has only seen one *Starglider* in pristine condition once before, when Ser Kodak opened the gate in the Helen System.

Abel circles the ship, examining the sails and the hull. He gently lays a hand on its surface. A quiet hum vibrates through his palm and forearm, as if it is divine.

"Beautiful, isn't it?" A voice rings out from behind. Abel whirls around and points the pistol in the direction of the voice. The outline of the man is speaking, yet the shadows cover his face.

"Just like how I remember it," Abel replies. The man's voice sounds so familiar, it itches Abel's mind.

The voice chuckles. "You don't need to point that. At least not yet."

The man emerges from the shadows, his black robes seem to blend in with the darkness. He holds a glossy black mask in his hands. Abel glances at the mask, then peers up at its owner and finds his own face staring back at him.

He gasps and steps back. Seeing his own face on another body is not a feeling that people are used to. Yet he shakes it off and lowers his pistol. "So, Kane," Abel starts. "Did you give yourself that name or did someone else give it to you?"

Kane chuckles, and his hands press together. "After I woke up from the wreckage on Uvir, I had no memory of who I was. Most of everything I knew, including the map that is now in your mind, had vanished. I learned everything about my past from recordings and archives I salvaged from the ship. After that, I knew I needed to hide. Gave myself that name, a new identity, and a new role. Many years passed and...here we are."

Abel tilts his head. He examines Kane's face, almost exactly like his. Except for the blister scars that Abel received on Aegis 12. The very thought causes Abel to rub the craters on his face. "Ah. I imagine Aegis left its mark. Tell me. The skull you found on that toxic world—do you remember that day?" Kane takes a step closer. "Do you remember how you hunted him down? How you tracked him for months?"

Abel nods. "Yes."

"How did it feel? When you finally caught him?"

Abel hasn't thought about tracking down memories of

alternate Abels to Aegis 12. Now he does. He followed his trail all the way to that cave and put a slugger in his skull. "It was like any other gig," Abel mutters.

"Ah. Another gig." Kane turns away from Abel and stares at the *Starglider*. "Amazing how you can have that mentality. Do you remember how he pled? How he begged? Because he was the only one out of all of us who hailed from the universe where his mother, *our* mother, was still alive." Kane's voice becomes sharper as he continues, and he turns to face Abel again.

"But you didn't listen. All he wanted was to go back home to his mother. To see her face. Despite that, you still ended him right then and there."

The weight of the memory presses down on his chest. He does remember how he begged; how he can see his own face through his E.V.A. helmet visor; how there were tears in the man's eyes. But he couldn't risk him using that knowledge to destroy worlds.

"Amazing how you stayed on mission." Kane says, his tone icy.

"I did what I had to," Abel retorts.

"Oh, you sure did. You hunted us all down, one by one. Eliminating Ser Kodak and suppressing your own memory. I could've used this knowledge on my own, but after the sabotaging you did, not even Kodak's memory-manipulator machine could bring it back."

"So, you're the only one who survived that wreckage on Uvir?"

"No guarantees, but there were many corpses there."

Abel gestures toward the ship. "So your plan is to fly this and open a new gate wherever you can find a large enough star? Then what?"

"I plan on continuing Ser Kodak's mission. Cyra was perhaps more dedicated than I. Yet with you standing here instead of her, I assume she is no longer with us?"

The sight of Cyra splattered by Abel's ship flashes back in his mind. He nods.

Kane's lips press together. "She was a most dedicated woman. Obsessed with fulfilling Ser Kodak's mission. Yet her obsession and hatred blinded her. She dedicated her whole life to fulfilling another man's dream. How foolish is that?"

"You tell me," Abel says. "You're the one who built all of this—this empire and even constructed the *Starglider*. I would say that is fulfilling another man's dream, if not your own."

"Perhaps you're right." Kane paces, his hands interlocked behind his back. "Or perhaps, you couldn't be more wrong."

"Excuse me?"

"Abel, you can't be that naive. Certainly you see that you've been trying to fulfill Kodak's legacy? You wear his coat for heaven's sake. You took one of his ships, and you took Cleo as a pet. You hunted us all down and even kept the memory of that map."

"No, I erased the memory of the map to further protect that knowledge." Abel raises his finger in defense.

Kane steps forward, their noses inches apart. "Yeah? Then tell me this. After you killed all of us, and you were certain that no one else had the map, why didn't you erase yourself as well?"

Abel smirks. "You're out of your mind."

"Am I?" Kane steps back. "If you're so dedicated to making sure no one could take advantage of you or that knowledge, why didn't you leave yourself to be swallowed on Aegis 12 after you killed that man? Perhaps you felt you wanted to use it someday."

"Or maybe I didn't want to die," Abel replies.

"Maybe. Ser Kodak taught us many things, but there was much he didn't teach us."

"What do you mean?" Abel tilts his head.

"Oh, Abel, you remember the details of his experiment." Kane chuckles underneath his words, then continues. "How he was willing to sacrifice universe upon universe, bend reality itself in order to construct the perfect one."

"The man was insane. I'm aware."

"Yet you think that he only wanted to apply that method to universes?"

Abel soaks in Kane's words. Did Ser Kodak have other experiments in mind? "What the hell do you mean?"

"Ser Kodak knew that he wouldn't live long enough to see the end of his mission. Only a fool would think that he would. Thus, he decided to apply that same philosophy on other variables."

"You'd better start making sense." Abel tightens his grip on his plasma pistol.

"Other variables, as in us." Kane answers, his face still as stone. "This is what he wanted all along. The best of us to rise, to take charge of his mission, even if that meant killing the other Abels." He lifts his hands.

Abel isn't sure how to respond. Is Kane as mad as Ser Kodak? Or is he the sanest out of all of them?

"I know what I've done, the terrible things I did to build this," Kane speaks softly. "But after all these years, it wasn't for me. It was for us."

The man may be crazy, but Abel recognizes the burden

that Kane also carries. He is a man who unknowingly lost his memory but has still made something out of himself. Both of them, victims of the ideology of a self-proclaimed messiah.

"for us?"

"Well, for one of us."

Abel grips his pistol tighter, but Kane doesn't make any sudden movements.

"You know how this ends," Kane says. "Only one of us can leave this hangar. Despite me taking a different name, the universe isn't large enough for the two of us. One of us must die. It is what he wants. What he has always wanted. For us to rise like he did. To squash those that oppose his mission, and to inherent this perfect universe. And it all starts with one of us leaving this hangar, and the other staying on the floor, lifeless."

A silent eternity passes. Abel stares at the plasma pistol in his hand, and Kane watches him process his thoughts. Ser Kodak didn't only want the perfect universe, he also wanted the perfect inheritor for his legacy. Even in death, Abel can still feel the strings from Ser Kodak's hands. Ser's influence will forever plague his existence. Abel can choose to give up and submit to the legacy, the mission. Become like Kane and Cyra, obsessed with fulfilling a seemingly divine prophecy. A goal that humanity can only dream about, yet can only achieve with great sacrifice.

No, Abel thinks to himself. No more. He points the pistol at Kane's forehead. Kane is unfazed by the sudden threat of his life.

"Ah yes." Kane closes his eyes and raises his arms. "Like he always wanted."

Yet a moment passes, and Kane remains standing, arms raised. When a shot doesn't ring out, he opens his eyes. Then his brow unfurrows. Abel is holding the pistol with the grip facing Kane.

"I don't understand."

"I'm done," Abel replies with a firm voice. "I'm done having the old man influence my life for some prophecy. I'm done living my life by his teachings, by his wishes. From this moment on, I refuse to fulfill his legacy. No more."

Their eyes lock, and Kane slowly takes the pistol away from Abel's grip. Abel lowers his hand and straightens his shoulders to face Kane, at this mercy for whatever happens next.

Kane gazes down at the plasma pistol. He looks up at Abel, then back down to the pistol. "Do you remember those words? The words Ser Kodak would always say?"

Abel recalls the many sayings of Ser Kodak, yet there's always one that rings louder than the rest. "The cost of fortune," Abel whispers.

Kane nods. "The cost of fortune."

This is it, then. The cost that Ser was referring to. "I think I understand it now," Abel says. "Whatever form that fortune takes, there is always an enormous cost."

Kane nods. "What is that fortune for you, Abel?"

He bows his head, becoming lost in his own thoughts. Despite Kane standing there with the weapon in his hand, no one has ever asked him this question before. Absolutely nobody. It catches him off-guard, causing a moment of existential crisis. The man with his face standing there with his gun—the irony isn't lost on him.

Is it wealth? Is it power? Is it enlightenment of some kind? Abel finds the answer amidst his thoughts. The one reason why he's never retired from the Collector's life. The one reason why he erased his memory to begin with.

"Freedom," Abel replies softly. "Freedom from everything."

Kane nods and even seems amused by Abel's answer. "With everything that has happened in the past few decades—This mind-bending legacy Ser Kodak has left us—one thing is for sure. You are the most free of all of us."

Abel can only stare, his face almost numb. Kane's words hit him like a thump in the chest. Then his heart sinks. Kane raises the pistol in a sudden motion.

A shot rings out throughout the entire hangar.

Chapter 25

"What is going on in there?" Vadim asks, annoyance dripping from each word.

"I told you this is between him and Kane," Eva snaps back from her seat, then picks at her cuticle.

"Why exactly do we have to wait out here, anyway?" Zao says. "Shouldn't we be helping him? He's facing a leader of a shadow organization. We should at least be watching what's going on."

"You wouldn't understand it," Eva states.

"And you would?" Zao snarks back.

"Enough." Vadim steps in, calm yet intimidating. "I understand when a man must fight his own battle. Abel's sole dealing with Kane—it's what he needs. We don't have to understand it. Instead, we should map out a plan for getting out of here, since you wrecked our way out."

"You're welcome for saving your life," Zao grouses.

Vadim snarls a lip at Zao while Eva sits with her knees up against her chest, staring at the interplay between the rising sun and the ever-present moon, along with the backdrop of meteors falling from the sky.

A man steps into the courtyard, catching everyone's attention. Zao and Vadim stop arguing at the man's presence. Eva turns at the echo of footsteps, and her breath hitches. A man approaches carrying a black mask.

At first her heart beats fast, then she sees Abel, still wearing his thick, smelly coat, still sporting blister scars on his face. Her fear transforms into relief.

"Abel," Zao calls out. "Nice of you to join us."

Even from a distance, his grin is apparent. He trudges toward them. Something is different—different in the man that had raided the estate. As he moved closer, Eva bolts toward him and examines him closer. Abel stops, startled by her sudden examination. Then she grabs him by the jaw and moves his head from side to side, examining his blister scars.

"Eva, relax. It's me," Abel murmurs. She backs off, wiping her hands on her coat.

"Sorry, can't be too careful. Is it over?"

Abel nods. "It's over."

Zao steps closer, scowling as usual. "What happened?"

Abel hands the mask to Zao. "He offed himself."

A deep groove forms between Zao's eyes. "What, why?"

Abel shrugs. "He couldn't see a way out, I suppose. Also, he was... well... tired."

"His body in the hangar?" Vadim asks.

"No, I tossed it out, off the cliff. He's not a problem anymore."

Vadim nods and turns toward the ruined estate. The other surviving Satyr militants are disposing of the bodies and zipping up the bags of their own dead. "All that expensive marble and wood, the shattered glass wall of the gallery and the ship crashing inside leave one hell of a mess.

Soon, this place will be a ruin. A site of another forgotten story." Vadim then turns toward the group. "Our duty here is finished. I'll take the other Satyrs."

Abel steps forward and extends a hand. "Thank you, Vadim. For everything."

Vadim stares at his hand, then meets his eyes. He grabs his hand in a firm shake. "Thank you for helping us accomplish our purpose and rescue Eva. Speaking of which—" He turns to Eva.

She snaps out of her usual trance. "Yes?"

"Would you like to come with us? We can still use you in our fight."

Abel and Zao stare at Eva. She presses her fingers toward her temples and thinks for a moment. Then her shoulders lower, and a smile lights up her face. She exchanges a glance with both of them, then turns toward Vadim. "This Collector life is charming. Maybe time for a career change?"

Vadim nods, and a half a grin plays on Abel's lips. Zao beams.

"Well, you know where to find us." Vadim spins at the sound of a Satyr militant calling out.

"Vadim, we found some ships close to the estate. Most likely the mercenary ships."

Vadim grins and steps back to leave. "Looks like that is my cue." With that, he joins the other Satyrs.

***

The three of them watch Vadim join the others and make their preparations to depart. Cleo hovers around in her hawk form.

"So," Abel turns to Eva. "You want to be a Collector now?"

Eva nods. "How does one get started? Zao told me that they usually are brought up by a mentor."

Abel raises an eyebrow. "Well, who says we can't start now?" He then turns to Zao. "So, got any leads for us?"

Zao's eyes widen from the question. "Oh, you mean now?"

"Yeah, why not?"

Zao rests his chin in his hand. "I do have one."

"Great. Where is—"

"On one condition." Zao raises his finger, cutting Abel off.

Abel sighs. "I'm guessing you want a higher cut now after all of this."

"No." Zao pauses and lowers his hand. "I want to come with you."

Abel is surprised, even pleasantly surprised. Zao has never been one to want to join him on a gig, but he has stuck with him through all of this, perhaps even saving the universe in the process. Abel grins. "Okay, but a little warning. We'll be doing things like climbing, running, staying in tight and dark spaces—just exercise in general."

"Oh, stop before you make me laugh hysterically," Zao replies with a straight face. "I know what I'm getting into. How am I supposed to return to my incense shop after all of this?" He waves his arm around the entire wrecked estate. "I'm coming with you. End of discussion."

Abel smiles and places his hand on Zao's shoulder. "Welcome to the team then."

Zao returns his smile. Zao then turns to Eva. "Time to find a way out of here. Shall we go see what ships they found."

"I know just the one," Eva replies. Zao and she head to a

hangar.

Abel finds himself standing in the courtyard alone, staring up into the sky. The moon is truly something else, just like he remembers it. He approaches the cliff of the courtyard, and familiarity strikes him yet again.

This is the cliff where he and Ethan first conversed when they set up camp, where Ethan planted the scanner. The memory strikes him in the chest of his youth, and he wishes he could've saved them. Perhaps things would've been different.

Abel sheds his coat, the one that once hugged the man named Ser Kodak. He holds it in his arms, feeling the cool winds pierce through his knitted shirt, feeling the fabric of the coat. Then he tosses the coat off the cliff, watching it free-fall into the canyon below.

Cleo hovers next to him, still in the shape of a hawk. Abel glances over to the spectral bird, feeling the winds brush against his face. For once, he feels relieved. He feels truly free.

That is until Cleo begins to act strangely, her holographic particles morphing. Abel takes a step back, cautious of what is happening in front of him, for he has never seen this before. "Cleo, are you okay?"

As in response, the particles take shape of a man who stands at the edge of the cliff with one hand behind his back, the other with a cigar. The particle colors change to simulate a live human standing before him. The man stands straight and looks off into the distance.

"Ser...Ser Kodak?" Abel's voice trembles, restraining his fist from punching the man. From pushing him off the cliff and watching him fall to his death. Yet the man who stands in front of him is only an illusion. A ghost of a once-powerful man.

"Abel—" Ser Kodak begins. "If you're seeing this, then you know which Abel I'm addressing."

Abel blinks his eyes rapidly. *What is this?*

"If you are seeing this, that means that you did it. You won. Like I predicted you would. You're probably wondering why I recorded this then, or how I predicted that you would be the last of us standing. It's because you are the only one who can carry this on."

Abel tilts his head, soaking in the words from a dead man. Carry what on?

"I made a mistake, Abel. A mistake that could threaten our reality. If you are the man that I think you are, then you're the only one that can correct this. That can save us all—"

Abel whispers under his breath. "What did you do?"

"The rifts that I have opened, including the one in the Helen system, are causing our reality to become unstable. Our universe is falling apart, taking the lives of billions, if not trillions, if it remains uncorrected. But they can be closed."

Closing a black hole? How can one do that?

"When I first discovered the possibility of opening rifts, I ventured into a ruin in my younger days. A cavern, much like the one where you found the obelisk. I became obsessed with the symbols and deciphering these ancient ruins. They eventually led me to these remarkable discoveries."

Abel, as in a trance, says, "What discoveries? Where are they?"

"I came to call them the Vaults of Eden, resting places for the ancient travelers of the universe. They're placed in key places in this universe, places where reality is flexible and unpredictable. Unpredictable anomalies, like the one that took Ethan's life."

Abel's heart sinks at the memory of Ethan's death.

"Abel, the Vaults of Eden hold the key to closing these rifts. You must find them, study them, and correct my wrongdoings. Free our universe from the grasp of the void, for you are the one with the knowledge to decipher the vaults. The knowledge is already inside you; you only need to reach out."

Abel is stunned. He can't believe what he is hearing. Ser Kodak's body morphs again. The particles shift and change, and Cleo displays the particles in an odd shape. Yet, he recognizes it almost immediately.

The particles shift into the symbols, like the ones he found down in the apparent Vault of Eden. Before touching the obelisk, he couldn't read these. Not even Cleo could find a basis for the language. Yet, now he can understand them as clear as English. The sudden understanding surprises him at first, then a shiver travels down his spine as he reads the symbols.

Hear us… Find us…

The End.

Gregory A. Dedicke, known to family and friends as "Greg", is a self-proclaimed "student of life" and driven entrepreneur. His passion for writing manifested at a young age and began with many fictional short stories, ultimately leading him to "Abel's Burden", his first published work. Greg co-founded, American Renegades, a lifestyle company focusing on the pursuit of freedom, adventure, and self-reliance. He currently lives in Niceville, Florida and has already begun crafting his next novel.

Made in the USA
Columbia, SC
24 August 2019